Mrs Kneebone and Me

Nora Dugon

Attic Press
DUBLIN

To Phillip and Margaret

First published in 1988 by University of Queensland Press under the title *Lonely Summers*.

This edition first published in Ireland in 1994 by
Attic Press
4 Upper Mount Street
Dublin 2

ISBN 1 85594 150 3

A CIP record for this title is available from the British Library

Cover Design: Angela Clarke
Printing: The Guernsey Press Co Ltd.

This book is published with the assistance of the Arts Council/An Chomhairle Ealaíon.

1

Mrs Kneebone met Kelly at a time when she was beginning to feel old. Although she could not remember a time when she had felt young she now noticed an unusual weariness was entering her bones. She was sensitive to draughts and, with her failing eyesight, she thought she saw dust on polished surfaces and cobwebs near the ceiling. At this time, when she had begun to wander through her empty house overcome by uncertainties, Kelly, the lost orphan, seemed to enter her life as a godsend.

"You watch out! She'll be big trouble that one!" warned Mrs Swann. Actually Kelly was very small. She claimed she was sixteen and had a birth certificate to prove it if she could only find it, but she didn't look a day more than twelve or thirteen.

"My father was a midget," she said when she measured herself against other girls of her age. She had no father: he died before she knew him. Her mother kept a photograph of him which showed a melancholy charm and the gentle, bearded face of a religious martyr. But even her mother had no real part in Kelly's first memories of a time when she had lived in a sort of farmhouse, cared

1

for by a woman she called *Gramma*. In those days her mother had been no more than a faint recollection of some sort of hippie who had gone to the mainland with her skirt tied up under her armpits. That woman had returned to Tasmania to claim Kelly years later, just before she was old enough to go to school. Since then Kelly had gone to many schools and her education had nothing to do with any of them. She learned to recognise the woman as her mother but always called her 'Peg'. Peg had taken Kelly back to the mainland and they had travelled here and there together. At first they went to a farm called a *commune* where Kelly discovered she had a lot of 'aunts' and 'uncles' she had never heard of before. Peg explained them as her 'extended family' and said this was the proper way to live with other people.

As she grew up, Kelly found difficulties in understanding her relationship to a whole lot of people, so she thought it was easier to tell Mrs Kneebone that she was an orphan. She wasn't the only kid Peg had collected and then abandoned along the way. Peg could become very attached to children and animals and other people for a short time. She was the sort of person everyone seemed to like, at least for a while. She appeared so simple and sympathetic, even silly at times; but there were hints of a frightening complexity. Although her attitude to life was, on the surface, communal and co-operative, she had inside her a separateness that led her from one relationship to another and from place to place. She floated through life as if she had no weight to hold her still, going on her way with her guitar and songs like a summer breeze that caressed and refreshed but could not be touched or held. Kelly went with her, up and down the east coast of the mainland until they had returned to Tasmania. Then Peg left Kelly behind. And Kelly found Mrs Kneebone.

Mrs Swann said that she could see that Mrs Kneebone was *quite taken* with the girl. *Surprisingly*, she said, although Mrs Kneebone was more surprised than anyone by her own action in taking Kelly into her house. Until then her life had been solitary and she had never known that she wished it to be otherwise. She herself had been orphaned at the age of sixteen when her parents were struck down by a brewery cart while crossing the road one dark, wintry night. After that Mrs Kneebone, vowing, because of the accident, never to touch a drop of alcoholic beverage, became a nurse, married a sick man and was a childless widow by the age of forty-five. Now over sixty, she would have been penniless as well without her pension.

"But I've still got my health," she would say. It was true that she suffered from nothing worse than being overweight and having high blood-pressure and arthritis. "And I've got my own home," she would add, comforted.

Kelly thought that Mrs Kneebone's house was *just lovely*: all that chintz and velvet, the comfort of deep-cushioned, sagging chairs; its air of permanency. In the luxury of old linen and eiderdown on that first night she had cried herself softly and warmly to sleep. She slept late into the next day while the old woman got up and wandered through the rooms, rearranging net curtains, antimacassars and porcelain ornaments. Waiting for the girl to wake up, Mrs Kneebone made a pot of tea and two slices of toast. She drank the tea and ate the toast, and still waited. After a while she made another pot of tea and took a cup to Kelly, who was still sleeping, as tender and vulnerable as a flower with her dark hair spread out over the pillow. Looking down at her, Mrs Kneebone found her hand was trembling as she set down the cup. Kelly started from her sleep and opened her eyes.

3

"My dear," murmured Mrs Kneebone reassuringly, "it's all right." She reached out her arms (had she been going to embrace the girl?) and then withdrew them quickly. Uncertain of emotion she drew back, afraid of wandering into some dangerous territory where disaster might await her. She could not guess how that disaster might come, but a strange fear touched her for a moment. She hurried back to her kitchen and had another cup of tea, trying to put the strange experience behind her and regain her usual sensible feelings.

Before Peg had left Kelly, they had stayed together in a house with a woman called Allie Jones. Allie carried the scars of domestic violence like a banner.

"Got them from Terry the Terrorist!"

Terry was her ex-husband. He hadn't had it all his own way, she said: she had broken a bottle over his head and left him with a knife scar in his side.

"Finished with him now," she said. "Gotta think of the kids. They're getting old enough to take sides and join the firing lines. We're out on our own now."

But they were not entirely on their own. Allie invited anyone who needed sanctuary to share her place. "Wouldn't turn away a kicked dog," she said. And she wouldn't. Allie was rough but kind. She never turned away from trouble, she said, and trouble knew it.

Kelly and Peg had ended up at Allie's place with some friends they had made at a folk festival in a country town just outside the city. "We can all crash at Allie's," they'd said.

"Yeh, any time," agreed Allie as they spread their sleeping-bags on the floor.

Allie's house was a wreck in a weed-ridden garden,

where everything was mildewed and worm-eaten to the final stages of decay.

"Anyone can drop in any time. If I'm not at home just lean on the back door and it'll fall in."

Kelly and Peg stayed on after the other folk festival people had gone. Allie's children watched Kelly warily. Mandy and Mick were about ten and twelve years old, the boy younger than the girl.

"How old are ya?"

"Sixteen," said Kelly.

"Ya don't look it."

"What do you know? You're only kids!" she told them.

"We know plenty," they told her.

They knew what grown-ups were like. They didn't reckon that Kelly was grown-up. They hung about, waiting for her to get undressed for bed. She heard them giggling when she was under the shower. She hated them. Mandy was sly and knowing, yet still childishly candid.

"Your mum's mad, isn't she?"

In spite of certain outward signs Kelly refused to admit this, although it was a possibility she was being forced to consider. The thought sometimes occurred to her: *Who is responsible*? She thought she could see the time coming when she would be the one to take care of her mother. Perhaps Peg had also seen this possibility when she left Kelly behind.

So Kelly woke up one morning to find Peg had gone.

"Your mum's forgot you," said Mandy.

It was the day after the incident in the antique shop on the main road. Peg and Kelly had been browsing about in there when a man came from the back of the shop to stand staring at Peg, who didn't notice him at first. It was Kelly who drew Peg's attention to the man. His mouth was open and there was a strange expression on

5

his face. He was old, with grey hair and grey skin. As soon as Peg saw him she grabbed Kelly by the hand and ran out of the shop, knocking over a couple of ornaments. Kelly heard them fall and break as they ran. The man followed, calling to them, but they ran without stopping until they were well away from the shop. Even then they walked quickly with Peg looking back all the time to make sure they were not being pursued.

"Why did we run?" asked Kelly when they were back at Allie's place.

"We broke something," said Peg.

"That was after we started running," Kelly pointed out.

But Peg only said, "We had to get away or we'd have had to pay for the breakages."

Kelly wondered if Peg had stolen anything from the shop. She knew that Peg was not a thief, not dishonest in any way in which she understood dishonesty. On the other hand, in their communal lifestyle Peg had often displayed an easy attitude to possessions. She did not regard possession as exclusive ownership; she had a tendency to share whatever was at hand. She saw giving and receiving as two sides of the one coin.

"Why did your mum go without you?" said Mandy.

"She'll come back."

"Maybe she forgot you."

Maybe, thought Kelly. Peg had forgotten things before; she'd come back. But when Peg hadn't come back after days of Mandy's questions and sly looks, Kelly decided there was no reason for her to stay at Allie's place any longer. Allie said there was no need for her to go either, she could stay as long as she liked.

"Maybe you've gotta learn to take care of yourself though," she added. "You should be getting social security, I reckon. It's worth trying. If you don't screw the system, it'll screw you."

"I can take care of myself," said Kelly.

Peg had tucked a few dollars into Kelly's sleeping-bag before she left. Kelly took this money to the local charity shop, looking for some decent secondhand clothes. If she was going to get a job to support herself, she would need to look less like a hippie. Mrs Kneebone was at the shop. She worked there every Thursday. She liked the company of the other women and the feeling of being useful to the *less fortunate*, although she had never actually defined those less fortunate than a solitary widow living alone on a pension in a damp, draughty old house.

"It's dollar day," said Mrs Kneebone cheerfully, smiling at Kelly. "Everything's a dollar today."

Kelly did not have many dollars, and she tried on a lot of clothes to decide how to spend her money. She saw that it was starting to rain outside, and was pleased to find a large rain-cape, the sort of thing bush walkers wore. She could camp out under that, she thought. It was late in the afternoon and Mrs Kneebone said they would be closing soon. Kelly collected an assortment of skirts, shirts and pants, and went into the little changing room. She could hear the rain on the windows and the iron roof. Somehow it made the little room seem cosy and secure. When she had made up her mind what she wanted to buy, Kelly sat there on the chair for a little while and thought about things. She could hear the two women moving about, talking in low voices, tidying up before closing the shop. Maybe if she stayed very quiet, thought Kelly, they would forget she was there. She had seen a little kitchen behind the counter with an electric jug and a small refrigerator; maybe there were some biscuits or something somewhere. She could make her-

7

self comfortable for the night here, and let herself out in the morning before anyone arrived.

Just then the door of the little room opened, and Mrs Swann looked in. "Are you still here?"

"What! Someone still there?" said Mrs Kneebone, also coming to look.

"I've lost my mother," said Kelly.

"What?"

"Where?"

"She's gone. I'm an orphan now."

"Poor little thing!" cried Mrs Kneebone.

"Where do you live?" asked Mrs Swann.

"Nowhere," said Kelly. Her grey eyes looked up from under a fringe of dark hair. She managed to look so abject and forlorn that Mrs Kneebone heard herself saying, "You'd better come home with me, love."

2

Mrs Swann took them home in her mini. Kelly gathered together the few pieces of clothing she had decided to buy, offering her few dollars to pay for them, which Mrs Kneebone refused to accept.

"Never mind about that!"

Mrs Kneebone was feeling very strange. She was surprised at herself, wondering about her own sudden decision to take this strange girl home with her. But she couldn't let her go out in the rain, could she?

At first Kelly thought they were heading back to Allie's place, then the mini turned off into Clare Street. This was a long street, which could be described as going downhill over the years. The houses were first built for working men employed on the docks or in nearby factories, but change was coming to Clare Street. The little houses, described by estate agents as *charming cottages*, due for demolition or renovation, could be bought and rented cheaply. Towards the city end, the long street was regarded as trendy. Young couples were moving in, painting and decorating, turning small dusty backyard gardens into *courtyards* with trellises covered in vines, where they gave wine-and-cheese parties, more *chic* and also cheaper than beer-and-beef barbecues. Mrs Knee-bone's house was a little more towards the decaying derelict than the trendy end of the street.

It could not have been classed as one of the charming cottages, but it had a well-tended garden, and with a coat of paint and a new fence and a few other repairs would have presented an appearance as respectable as Mrs Kneebone herself. It had lace curtains and flowers in the front windows, the garden beds were weeded, the grass and hedge neatly clipped. Beyond Mrs Kneebone's house, down the unfashionable end, most of Clare Street's residents were supported by pensions or welfare benefits, paid by the government. It could also be said that the residents at the trendy end were supported by the government, as most of them were employed in the Public Service. In spite of the fact that they were, in a way, all paid from the same purse, the trendy inhabitants of Clare Street tended to look down upon the inhabitants of the other end.

A couple who regarded themselves as an exception to the general rule lived right at the city end of Clare Street. Timothy and Frieda Towns, former teachers, had saved their money, given up their jobs, and bought a cottage to renovate. Timothy Towns had also bought, very cheaply, a half-share in a secondhand shop which he was turning into an antique business just round the corner from Clare Street, on the main city road. His wife Frieda, known to everyone as Fred, was doing most of the renovating of their house. She used what she called *earthy* colours such as reddish browns and plum, and tawny yellow and *vert antique* in her paints and furnishings, with unusual and not altogether disastrous results. Everyone agreed their house was different.

The Towns said they were not snobs and tried to be

friendly with everyone they met. Indeed, they went out of their way to meet everyone in Clare Street.

"You never know what might be lying about in some of those old houses," said Timothy. He had visions of walking nonchalantly into the houses and offering *amazing* prices (but well below market value) for what the owners regarded as bits of old junk. He would be seen as a benefactor in Clare Street and a man with an eye for a good bargain in the antique market. Fred thought the people of Clare Street were just *far out* and such an *absolutely fantastic cross-section* of society that she wanted to get to know everybody.

Mrs Kneebone thought that Mrs Towns was too interested in everybody else's business, and pretended not to see her when she waved to them as they drove past in Mrs Swann's mini the day Kelly came to Clare Street. Fred Towns then moved right out into the middle of the street and waved again, so that Mrs Kneebone, out of old-fashioned politeness, was forced to return the salutation. Fred Towns stayed there, watching as Mrs Swann's mini pulled up and Mrs Kneebone and Kelly got out and went into Mrs Kneebone's house. She was too far away, however, to get a good look at Kelly. Later she said to Timothy, "That old Kneebone woman must have her granddaughter staying with her."

"Didn't know she had any grandchildren. Didn't think she had any kids," said Timothy. "I wouldn't mind having a look into her house one day," he added.

"It's easier to get to know people through children," Fred observed.

Kelly had never seen anything like Mrs Kneebone's house before. There was scarcely room to move in it. Mrs Kneebone said it had been left to her by her husband, who had lived there all his life. It was stuffed with relics and heirlooms of his family: furniture, pictures, bric-a-brac of all sorts. Mrs Kneebone showed Kelly into a small bedroom at the back.

"I hope you like it."

"It's lovely!" breathed Kelly, who had never seen anything so pretty and creamy and chintzy in her life.

"I hope you'll be comfortable here," said Mrs Kneebone.

Kelly loved the whole house, the security of rooms unchanged for a lifetime, stuffed with things gathered and kept intact over the years, not broken or discarded or forgotten when people moved on. On the other hand, although there were clear signs that the house had been inhabited by a single line of occupants for over half a century, containing much evidence of the departed, there was no sign that the past had relinquished anything to the present or the future. After a few days it began to seem to Kelly more like a museum than a home. She went back to visit Allie, who shooed her out because she was holding a crisis meeting of local inhabitants in the kitchen. Allie held a lot of crisis meetings in her kitchen. Kelly went down the back yard where Mick and Mandy were pulling a plank off the back shed to make a seesaw.

"Are ya really gonna live with a funny old woman?" they wanted to know.

"She's not real old," said Kelly.

"I bet she's over sixty."

"If she's a hundred," said Mick, "she'll get a telegram from the Queen."

"Big deal!" scoffed Mandy.

"Anyway," said Kelly, "she's nowhere near a hundred."

"How old is she? Seventy? Eighty?"

"I don't know."

"Why d'ya wanna live with an old woman? And why

12

d'ya wanna live in snobby Clare Street?" asked Mandy.

"It's not snobby where Mrs Kneebone lives."

"It's snobby where the Towns live," declared Mick. "Dad knows Timothy Towns. Do you know him?"

"What does he look like?"

"He looks like a poofter!" Mandy said, giggling.

"Dad wouldn't talk to him if he was a poofter!"

"He owns the secondhand shop, but it's an antique shop now."

"Is he an old guy?" asked Kelly, remembering the old man her mother had run away from.

"Nah! The old guy's the bloke that used to own the secondhand shop. He's still there, but this guy Towns is running the place now."

Kelly was not interested in the antique shop. "I'll have to get my sleeping bag and things."

"Ya goin' campin' or somthin'?"

"No, I just want my things," said Kelly. "But you never know," she added. It was all right at Mrs Kneebone's place, but nothing was ever certain. "I don't suppose I'll be living there forever."

"Yar not gonna live forever," said Mick. "They'll drop the bomb."

"What bomb?"

"Didn't ya see it on television? Everythin' that didn't get finished by the bomb got wiped out in the fire. Then there was flyin' glass 'n' everythin'! An' all the smoke 'n' stuff went up roun' the sun. It was like night fer years 'n' years. Everything died."

"When?"

"On the telly. It's gonna happen."

"When's it gonna happen?"

"I dunno. But cockroaches and rats won't get killed, Ya can't kill cockroaches and rats."

"You'll be orright then, won't ya?" said Mandy.

13

Mick punched her, and she grabbed his arm, twisting it behind his back. They rolled on the dusty grass together, punching each other.

"I'm going," said Kelly.

Allie stopped her on her way out. The crisis meeting was over. "Come to get your stuff, have you?"

Kelly said she had, and Allie helped her collect it.

"Did you really wanna go home with one of them holy Joannas?" Allie asked her.

"She's all right," said Kelly. "She's a nice woman."

"Not queer or anything, is she?"

"Of course not," said Kelly, although she was not sure that she knew what Allie meant. "She's very kind. And she's got a real nice house."

"I've seen her house," said Allie. "It needs a bit o' renovating. But I don't suppose I should criticise." She pulled a strip of peeling paint off the wall, then walked down the shaky front steps to the gate that was falling off its hinges. She looked at Kelly, anxiously. "I dunno what got into your mum to go and leave you like that."

"She forgets things," said Kelly.

"Has she forgotten you before?"

"Yeh, sometimes." Kelly shrugged. "But usually only for a couple of hours."

Allie shook her head. "If she comes back looking for you I'll tell her where you are. So you keep in touch with me, and let me know what you're doing. And if you need anything, any help or anything, or somewhere to shack up, you've always got this place."

"Thanks," said Kelly. She walked away with a warm feeling of gratitude. She had somewhere to stay and somewhere to go. Things could be worse.

3

Mrs Kneebone was touched by the pitifully small bundle of Kelly's possessions. "I can see we'll have to get you some things," she said, uncertain of the sort of things a teenage girl might need. "Is there anything you want?"

"I don't think so." Kelly worried about having more possessions than she could comfortably carry round with her. "But I might need some Tampax or something this week," she said, practically.

Mrs Kneebone blushed. "We'll have to get you some." She looked at Kelly, sadly. The child seemed so young. But the girl must pick up the woman's burden, she thought. Someone had once said that to Mrs Kneebone herself. Her mother, perhaps. It seemed such a long time ago. She had been frightened and unprepared for the burden. Now it was something she had quite forgotten. How quickly time passed.

Time did not pass quickly for Kelly, however, at Mrs Kneebone's place. It was difficult to tell it was passing at all, to distinguish one day from another. Except for Thursdays. On Thursday Mrs Kneebone worked at the charity shop. On her first Thursday with Mrs Kneebone, Kelly went there with her. Kelly thought the shop a marvellous place, an exciting jumble of all sorts of things. Racks of secondhand clothing stood in the centre of the floor, and around the walls were shelves of books and toys, ornaments, kitchenware, pictures, plastic flowers, boxes of baby clothes, odd cutlery, saucepan lids, buttons, bottle-tops. The place was busy all day, mostly with women and girls and young children, but some old men and teenage boys came in looking for clothing and other things, messing up the shelves, so that Kelly spent most of the day tidying up. It would be dead easy to pinch anything, she thought. You could just put it in your bag, or even put it on and walk out.

There was also a glass display-case in the shop, with silver, jewellery and small ornaments in it, which was kept locked. The things in there were more expensive.

"They're very good things," Mrs Kneebone told Kelly. "Almost antiques, some of them."

"Why don't you sell them at the antique shop?" asked Kelly.

"Oh, we couldn't do that!" exclaimed Mrs Kneebone. "They're given to us to sell here. And it's lovely just to see the expression on the face of someone who really appreciates them. They're so grateful to get something nice for a couple of dollars."

"Does the man from the antique shop ever come in and buy them?"

"Oh! he wouldn't do that!"

Kelly wondered how Mrs Kneebone was so sure that he wouldn't, but she didn't ask.

Later a man did come in and look closely at the things in the cabinet, but he wasn't Timothy Towns. Kelly thought he looked familiar, however; he reminded her of someone. He was handsome in a rough, thickset way, but he had that dissipated look she had learned to associate with drunkards or potheads. The man smiled ingratiatingly at Mrs Kneebone, and asked if he could look at one or two things in the cabinet. Mrs Kneebone unlocked the door, and the man took out one of the objects, fingering it carefully and lovingly.

"It's my wife's birthday," he told Mrs Kneebone. "I want to get her something nice, but I'm not working just now." He took out several things and looked at them. "I just can't make up my mind."

"Take your time," said Mrs Kneebone.

At that moment Kelly saw Mandy's brother, Mick, come into the shop. He looked surprised to see Kelly. "I didn't know you'd be here."

"What do you want?" she asked.

Mick shrugged and looked around. "Gotta pair o' shoes?"

"Oh, I'm sure we have," said Mrs Kneebone, who was suddenly hovering over them. "Is this a friend of yours, Kelly?

"Sort of," Kelly admitted.

Mick said he wanted a pair of joggers.

Mrs Kneebone searched through a box of assorted shoes. Mick was fussy about the colour: he wanted brown ones. Kelly noticed that the brown pair he selected had two dollars marked on the soles. He put them on and walked about, springing up and down, kicking at imaginary footballs.

"They're two dollars," said Kelly.

"A dollar for a friend of yours," said Mrs Kneebone.

Mick handed over a dollar coin, and walked out wearing the joggers and carrying his thongs.

By this time the man who had been looking at the things in the glass cabinet was waiting at the counter with a small porcelain bowl in his hand.

"So," Mrs Kneebone smiled at him indulgently, "you've decided, have you?" She looked at the price sticker. "Only a dollar fifty, and so pretty." She wrapped it in special gift paper and handed it over with a pamphlet about mothers' meetings held at the church hall. "Your wife might like to come. We have afternoon tea. Everyone's very friendly."

The man thanked her. "The wife doesn't go out much, but I'm sure she'd like to come."

As he left the shop Mrs Kneebone gazed after him, sighing in sympathy. "A secondhand present. Such a shame!" She went to lock the cabinet door. "Anyway," she said, putting the key back behind the counter, "I'm sure she'll like it."

Watching the man pass the window after he had left the shop, Kelly realised why he had seemed familiar: he looked like Mick. He could have been Mick's dad, she thought. But if he had been Mick's dad, surely they would have said something to one another. They had not looked as if they even recognised each other.

It was Mrs Swann who discovered that several items were missing from the glass case.

"Was it opened today?" she asked.

"Just once," said Mrs Kneebone. "But the man bought a little bowl, and *paid* for it."

"He might have taken something he didn't pay for," said Kelly.

"Oh, I don't think so!" cried Mrs Kneebone. "I'm sure he didn't!"

Then she realised that she was not sure. She had been busy at the time, attending to that friend of Kelly's.

Mrs Swann looked sharply and suspiciously at Kelly. "Several things are missing. A silver brooch, a butter knife, a pill-box, a chain."

"He seemed such a nice man!" said Mrs Kneebone. "It was his wife's birthday."

"You can't trust anyone," said Mrs Swann, still looking at Kelly. "Not these days."

Mrs Kneebone thought she couldn't go through life not trusting anyone.

"Oh well," said Mrs Swann, who did not want to worry Mrs Kneebone, "it's no use fussing about it, or calling the police. They never do anything. We'll just keep an eye open for him in future. And we must remember never to leave anyone alone by the cabinet when it's unlocked."

Remembering the look Mrs Swann had given her, and how upset Mrs Kneebone had been, Kelly went out after tea that evening, while it was still daylight, looking for Mick. She found him at home, took him down to a corner of the garden, and pushed him up against the fence so hard there was a danger that the fence would fall over. "Tell me the truth or I'll bust your head," she warned. She was not much bigger than Mick, but she knew he was no hero although he talked and swaggered a lot. He was used to being intimidated by Mandy.

"Was that guy your dad?"

"What if he was?"

"*Was he*?"

"Yeh, orright, he was! But he paid, didn't 'e?"

"Not for everything," said Kelly. "And you deliberately distracted attention, didn't you? You didn't even pay the proper price for your joggers, you little squirt!"

"So waddaya gonna do?"

"This time maybe I won't do anything," said Kelly.

Mick looked relieved.

"Only don't bet on it!" she added, giving him another shove against the fence.

"It won't happen again," promised Mick.

"I'll bust your head open if it does," said Kelly. "And I'll get the police on your dad!"

She left Mick leaning against the fence, and ran away through the garden, ignoring Mandy who appeared at a back window to shout after her, "Hi, Kelly! How're the Holy Joannas!"

4

As Kelly hurried down Clare Street, she saw Fred Towns on her front verandah.

"Hello. You're Mrs Kneebone's granddaughter, aren't you?"

Kelly thought that Mrs Towns probably knew very well that she was not Mrs Kneebone's granddaughter, so she avoided the question. "I'm just staying with her."

"It must be nice for her to have someone to stay with her. Especially someone young." Fred Towns smiled very brightly at Kelly, at the same time opening the gate to the verandah at the top of steps. "You look so hot! Have you been running?"

"Yes," mumbled Kelly, edging away. The woman looked ready to pounce on her and drag her inside.

Mrs Towns did not actually pounce, but she insisted, with her hand outstretched, "Come in and have a cool drink."

Kelly still edged away. "Aw, I dunno."

"I won't bite you," promised Mrs Towns, although it wouldn't have surprised Kelly if she had. She looked quite wolfish, standing at the open verandah gate, reaching out, smiling, eyes and teeth flashing. "Come on!"

Kelly saw that she could not refuse without being rude, so she went in, hesitating on the verandah, wondering if there was still time to get away. But Fred Towns was right behind her, closing the gate.

"Come inside. It's cool in the kitchen."

As Kelly followed her down the hall she said, "This house must be just like your grandmother's — I mean Mrs Kneebone's house."

"Sort of," said Kelly.

The Towns house had been originally designed like Mrs Kneebone's, but now it was very open and bright, although in contrast to Mrs Kneebone's house it seemed stark and cold.

"But it's different," said Kelly.

"Do you like carrot-and-apple juice?" asked Fred, opening the door of the refrigerator.

"Yes, thanks."

Fred filled two long glasses and handed one to Kelly. "Didn't I see you at Allie Jones's place the other day?"

"Maybe," said Kelly, taking a long drink.

"I was at a meeting there," said Fred Towns.

"Crisis?" asked Kelly.

Fred laughed. "I suppose it was. I suppose there are a lot of crises meetings at Allie's place."

Kelly said nothing. She was drinking her juice. She wondered what meeting Mrs Towns would have gone to at Allie's place. It couldn't have been for deserted wives or single mums. She looked into her glass, wondering if Allie ever held meetings for deserted kids.

"It was a meeting to form a local Neighbourhood Self-help Organisation," said Fred. "You wouldn't believe it, but some people think it's going to threaten them in some way."

Kelly looked up from her glass at Fred Towns. She had seen a lot of *self-helpers* in her time: she figured that

Mick and his dad were two of them. She gave a long sigh and put her glass down on the table.

"Like another one?" asked Fred.

"Thanks," said Kelly. "It's nice."

"Freshly made," said Fred, pouring out two more glasses of the drink.

"Mum used to make it," said Kelly, "when we lived in the Ashram."

Fred Towns looked startled. "Where?"

"A sort of religious place." Kelly picked up her glass and had a long drink. "Buddhist or something. It was good there. Everybody was nice."

Mrs Towns looked at her for a moment. Kelly knew she wanted to ask her some questions, but instead she just said, "Do you like carrot cake?"

"Love it!" said Kelly. "Mum used to make that too."

Fred Towns took the cake out of an old Arnott's biscuit tin, and cut several generous slices.

"Mum and me are really vegetarians," said Kelly.

Fred Towns put one of the large slices of cake on a small white plate.

"But it's not always easy to stick to it living with other people," Kelly added, biting into the dark, moist cake. "Hey, that's nice! Thanks!"

"Is Mrs Kneebone a vegetarian?" asked Fred. She was settling back for a long informative conversation.

"No, not really. She doesn't eat much at all."

"But she's quite a stout woman."

"Yeh. She eats a lot of toast."

"Anyway," said Fred Towns, "your mum sounds as if she had the right ideas about food."

"She liked a lotta raw stuff. It's easier that way when you're moving about."

"You move about a lot?"

"A bit."

"Where's your mum now?"

Kelly hesitated, quickly swallowed the last mouthful of cake, and said, "I lost her."

"Oh!" Fred Towns was touched, suddenly grieved.She had a good heart. "Is she dead?"

Kelly stood up. "I have to go now. Thanks." She put down her plate beside her empty glass, very neatly, not looking at Mrs Towns. "Mrs Kneebone will be expecting me."

Mrs Towns went down the hall with Kelly, and opened the verandah gate. "Now that we know each other you must drop in and see me whenever you want to."

Kelly, hesitating on the steps, wondered if she could get to like Mrs Towns. Then she ran down the street.

Later, talking to her husband, Fred said, "She's an interesting kid."

"Who?"

"That girl staying with Mrs Kneebone."

"I bet that's an interesting house inside," said Timothy. "There must be some good junk in there."

Fred nodded. "I should drop in and see her sometime. Take her a bit of carrot cake. Or maybe a vegetable pie or something."

Timothy poured a glass of beer for himself. He wasn't *into* vegetable or fruit juice, not after a day at work. "Got some nice pieces in today."

"Where from?"

"Terry whatever-his-name-is."

"Not Allie's ex? He's a brute!"

"I'll bet Allie is too," said Timothy, taking a long swallow of beer.

Fred giggled. "She's flattened him more than once — by her own accounts."

24

"Anyway," said Timothy, "Allie's Terry or not, he brought me in a few nice little pieces today."

"Where did he get them?"

"Who knows? The price was right and that's okay with me. There must be a lot of good stuff round here if you could get your hands on it."

"And apparently Terry does get his hands on it."

"Are you implying that he's not honest?"

"I'd be surprised if he was. What do you think?"

"I don't."

"So, Mrs Towns asked you in for a cold drink and a piece of cake," said Mrs Kneebone. "I wonder why she did that."

"Just being friendly, I suppose," said Kelly.

"What did she give you drink?" Mrs Kneebone sounded suspicious.

"Carrot-and-apple juice. She made it herself. You could make it. You've got a juice extractor. In the kitchen."

"Oh, *that*. It's been there for years."

A lot of things in that house had been there for years, thought Kelly. She wondered if some of them had ever been used.

"I used it to make juice for my husband," said Mrs Kneebone. "He was an invalid, you know."

"I could make juice with it," said Kelly.

"Yes, I suppose so." Mrs Kneebone sounded doubtful.

"I could make use of a lot of the stuff you've got round here. Out in the garden. Ever make mint tea or dandelion coffee?"

Mrs Kneebone gave a faint shudder.

"Or cucumber and daisy salad," Kelly went on. "Chop

up daisy leaves with mint and cucumber and crushed garlic. It's very good for you."

Even if it *was* good for you, thought Mrs Kneebone, she would rather have a Devonshire tea with scones and cream. But she didn't say anything.

"And daisies are good for your skin, especially spots." Kelly looked at Mrs Kneebone's mottled old hands. "You just wash the leaves and put them on your skin, then drink a cupful of daisy tea three times a day."

Mrs Kneebone was astonished. "Really? You wouldn't think daisies were so useful."

"Daisy leaves can even cure mouth ulcers," said Kelly.

"Well, I must remember that," said Mrs Kneebone, but she thought she would remember it for a long time before she tried it.

"My mum's really into herbs," said Kelly, then corrected herself quickly. "At least, she *was*."

"She must have been very clever," said Mrs Kneebone.

Kelly wasn't sure about that. "A lot of people thought she was a bit of a nut."

"*Really*, Kelly!" Mrs Kneebone admonished her. "You shouldn't say things like that about your mother!"

"But I like nuts, don't you?" Kelly smiled fondly at the old woman, and quite suddenly she felt sad. Where was Peg now? What was she doing? "Has she remembered me yet?" she wondered.

"Let's have some toast," said Mrs Kneebone.

"I'll make it," said Kelly.

Out in the kitchen, Kelly wondered how Peg was getting on without her. *Could* Peg get along without her? A woman who could forget her own daughter, thought Kelly, might forget anything. "And who's going to look after her but me?" she thought.

She took a plate of toast into the sitting room, and saw Mrs Kneebone looking up at her, smiling, peering through her scratched spectacles. "Geez!" though Kelly. "The world must be full of people who need looking after!" Another feeling of sadness almost overwhelmed her, and she had to hold back the tears.

But Mrs Kneebone said happily, "I've just had a lovely idea!" She was holding a small musical instrument in her hand. "Do you know what this is?"

"Sure. It's a recorder," said Kelly.

"Can you play it?"

"I reckon," said Kelly. "But I play a guitar better."

"I haven't got a guitar," said Mrs Kneebone. "You'll have to play this." Then, as if that was settled, she went on, "I'll play the piano. When my husband was alive, he used to play the recorder. He was fond of music. He used to be very happy sometimes, in spite of everything. I'd play the piano for him — something we could sing. I haven't bothered much since . . . Well, on my own . . . "

"Come on! I'll play the recorder," said Kelly quickly, putting the plate of toast aside.

Mrs Kneebone beamed. "I only play by ear."

She played 'Danny Boy', accompanied by Kelly, and then began 'The Black Velvet Band'. "Do you know this one?"

Kelly began to sing:

> "*Her eyes they shone like diamonds,*
> *You'd think she's the queen of the land.*
> *With her hair flung over her shoulders,*
> *Tied up with a black velvet band.*"

Mrs Kneebone said Kelly had a lovely voice. "It's a real *Irish* voice."

"Well, I suppose it ought to be," said Kelly. "My dad was Irish."

"What was he like?"

"I never saw him, so I don't remember him," said Kelly. "But Mum had a picture of him. He looked like Jesus Christ."

27

"Oh!" Mrs Kneebone wondered if that was blasphemy, but all she said was, "Let's have something bright now!"

She began to play 'Rum Tiddley', and sing in a high, cracked voice:

"Rum tiddley, um tiddley, um te tum,
What a bright little funny little tune!
Rum tiddley, um tiddley, um te tum,
You'll be singing it very soon.
I can't think where I heard the thing,
I know it made me want to sing,
Rum tiddley, um tiddley, um te tum,
What a funny little tune."

Kelly laughed. "I've never heard that one before!"

"My Alec loved it," said Mrs Kneebone, "That and 'Old MacDonald Had a Farm'. He liked to sing all the funny farm animal sounds. That was while he could sing. Or even listen. After a while he couldn't stand any sound at all. In the end I don't think he noticed anything. It was just as if he wasn't there at all." She looked at her hands on the piano and realised that it was the first time she had spoken about Alec like that to anyone. Usually she kept her personal feelings to herself.

Kelly began to sing:

"When you walk in the valley alone,
You will hear my lonely cry.
From far beyond the land of dreams,
As the lonely summers go by."

"This is one of my father's songs," she explained.

"When you hear the wind in the trees,
And you see the wild birds fly,
You will know I'm there by your side,
As the lonely summers go by."

Mrs Kneebone sighed. "That was lovely! Sometimes I feel that Alec is there like that. Do you feel that about your father?" Kelly didn't feel like that about her father. She had never known him.

"Have you any of his music? Any photographs?"

"No. Mum took all that stuff with her," said Kelly.

"Took it?" said Mrs Kneebone. She looked at Kelly. Their eyes met. "Where is your mother, dear?"

Kelly swallowed hard. "I don't know."

"Well," said Mrs Kneebone, irrationally not wanting to know, "I'm sure everything will be all right." She was not sure what she meant by that, but she was sure that things would be *all right*, she told herself, if Kelly stayed there with her. She could look after Kelly.

They had tea and toast and jam. Mrs Kneebone tried to make everything seem happy and bright. She played 'The Wild Colonial Boy' and 'Greensleeves' and 'Michael Row the Boat Ashore', and insisted on Kelly playing and singing with her. They ended with a rollicking chorus:

"There are no flies on us,
There are no flies on us.
There may be flies on some of you guys,
But there are no flies on us!"

Kelly went to bed thinking about Peg and the strange life they had lived together. She was restless for a long time before she fell asleep.

As for Mrs Kneebone, she lay awake too, thinking of her Alec and how she had mothered him through his long illness. Would she be allowed to mother Kelly now? Finally she went to sleep, only to be awakened again by the noise of people along the street talking and laughing, getting into cars and slamming doors. Such sounds had often disturbed Mrs Kneebone in the night. Usually they left her lying in the dark feeling lonely and excluded. Tonight they came to her with a feeling of warmth and neighbourliness; she had this silly idea that she would like to open the window and call out a cheerful *good-*

29

night, waving to the departing guests. Instead she very sensibly stayed in bed hugging her contentment to herself and recalling the pleasant evening with Kelly at the piano.

Kelly stirred in her sleep at the sound of the voices in the street. Had someone called her? She thought she heard the name *Colleen*. It was what her mother had called her when she was a very little girl. Sitting up in bed, she whispered, "Peg? Is that you?" But there were only the sounds of departure along the street, and she lay down again with her face buried in the pillow.

The Hoppers waved to their guests as they drove away. Before going inside again, Helen Hopper looked along Clare Street at all the little old houses, their shabbiness hidden under the cover of night.

"I'll be glad when they're all sold and renovated," she said to Lionel, her husband.

"There are advantages and disadvantages, getting in early on a redevelopment," Lionel said. "You've still got some of the old people who want to cling to their houses."

Fred Towns turned over in their big bed and said to Timothy, "Hoppers have had another dinner party. They've never invited us. But I've had them here at our wine and cheese evenings."

"Umph," said Timothy, and rolled over.

Fred thought about the Hoppers and decided that they were snobs.

"I don't think Helen Hopper wants to join our local self-help organisation because it would include *everybody*. *She* wants some sort of *exclusive club*."

"Umph," said Timothy, and rolled over again and pulled the pillow over his head.

Around the corner, on the main road, the old man who lived at the back of the new antique shop, which used to be his old secondhand shop, was troubled with sleeplessness and aches in his bones. He sat down in the kitchen with a mug of hot milk to which he had added a good measure of whisky. Already slightly maudlin with drink, he rubbed tears from his face with the sleeve of his pyjama coat. Softly he began to sing to himself:

> *"When you walk in the valley alone,*
> *You will hear my lonely cry.*
> *From far beyond the land of dreams,*
> *As the lonely summers go by."*

It was a song he always sang when he was feeling sentimental: it reminded him of his wife and son.

> *"When you hear the wind in the trees,*
> *And you see the wild birds fly,*
> *You will know I'm here by your side,*
> *As the lonely summers go by."*

5

Mrs Kneebone said she couldn't remember such a week: people coming and going every day. The first to arrive was Fred Towns, early in the morning, bearing a covered tray wreathed in the scent of herbs and spices and home-baking.

"I was just baking a carrot cake when I thought of Kelly," she said.

"Oh," said Mrs Kneebone, "why was that?"

"Well, Kelly loves carrot cake, doesn't she?" Fred lifted the cover from the tray.

"Does she?" said Mrs Kneebone, surprised. She saw that the tray held not only carrot cake but brown bread and a hot pie.

"And as she's a vegetarian, I thought I'd bake her a vegetable pie."

"A vegetarian?" Mrs Kneebone wondered where Mrs Towns got this information from. "She's never said anything to me."

"Well, you know," said Fred, "some people think vegetarians are a bit strange, and I don't supose she wanted to put you to any extra trouble."

"Kelly's no trouble at all," said Mrs Kneebone, suddenly feeling resentful.

Fred Towns had taken a seat at the kitchen table without being asked and was looking about the kitchen, taking in the colonial antiques on the pine dresser: plates in floral and willow pattern, creamware, silver salts and peppers, a pair of Mason octagonal jugs, an earthenware tureen . . .

"Wow!" said Fred Towns after taking a long breath. "You've got some lovely stuff here."

Lovely? Mrs Kneebone looked at her kitchen as if for the first time. She was aware of dust and dry rot.

"Everything belonged to my husband's family. It's very old."

"It's lovely," said Fred. Her eyes had turned very bright and greedy. As she seemed to have settled herself in the kitchen, Mrs Kneebone asked: "Would you like a cup of tea?"

"I'd love one," said Fred, and asked if Mrs Kneebone had any jasmin or herbal tea.

Mrs Kneebone shook her head. "Only ordinary Bushells." As she made the tea in her beautiful china pot, she was suddenly ashamed of her old kitchen and of not having any special tea; ashamed, too, of not knowing that Kelly was a vegetarian. Why hadn't Kelly told her?

"But I'm not," said Kelly, when Mrs Kneebone asked her about it later. "Only sometimes."

Mrs Kneebone felt aggrieved. "You should have told me."

"Why?" Kelly couldn't understand. "It doesn't matter, does it? I don't care what I eat."

But Mrs Kneebone could see how much she enjoyed the vegetable pie.

"I'd never have thought of making vegetable pie," she told Kelly. They were having lunch, as usual, in the kit-

33

chen. There was no dining-room in the cottage; Mrs Kneebone had all her meals in the kitchen. Except on those rare occasions when she had special guests. Then she would use the oval walnut table with the balloon-back chairs in the lounge-room. In the morning, when Fred Towns had sat down so confidently at the kitchen table, Mrs Kneebone had not known how to move her to the other room. Mrs Towns had not behaved like a guest at all, coming in through the back door, sitting down and making herself at home in the kitchen. It was as if the young woman had established some sort of relationship between them without agreement. Mrs Kneebone wasn't sure if she felt pleased or annoyed about it.

When Mandy and Mick started turning up at Mrs Kneebone's house, Kelly said to them, "I told you not to come here."

"But why shouldn't your friends come?" said Mrs Kneebone.

"They're not friends," said Kelly. "Just some kids."

"Well, they can come whenever they want to," said Mrs Kneebone. She approved of children, but like many childless women was slightly intimidated by them. She couldn't have prevented them from coming into her house. Mick came more often than Mandy. His sharp eyes took in everything. And Kelly watched him.

"You try to nick anything here and I'll kill you," she warned him when Mrs Kneebone was out of earshot.

"Me?" Mick looked at her, round-eyed and innocent.

It seemed to Kelly that Mrs Kneebone actually liked Mick. She even listened to his mad jokes.

"Didja hear about this goalkeeper nicknamed Cinderella? He kept missing the ball. Didja hear about the Irish Olympic Athlete who was given a dope test? He passed."

Mrs Kneebone looked more confused than amused, but she smiled nevertheless, because she knew the little

34

boy was trying to entertain her. Mick felt encouraged to go on.

"Show me a man that smiles in defeat and I'll show you a happy chiropodist."

"Oh, shut up!" Mandy gave her brother a shove. "Don't take any notice of him," she said to Mrs Kneebone. "He was born stupid, and he's had a relapse."

Mick made a face at her. "Why don't you keep Tasmania tidy? Stay in bed!"

Mandy didn't make corny jokes, but she asked endless questions. Did Mrs Kneebone have a husband? What did he die of? Did they have any kids? "Wotta ya knittin'? Why d'ya work in the op-shop? Can I pick some flowers in yer garden for me mum?"

Mrs Kneebone anwered her questions patiently.

Mandy asked Mrs Kneebone if she knew there were Vietnamese people in the fruit shop round the corner now. "Me dad has these problems because he was in Vietnam," she said.

Mrs Kneebone was sympathetic. Later, visiting Allie, Kelly remarked, "I didn't know Mandy's father was in Vietnam."

"Neither did I," Allie said.

"She's a dingdong liar," said Kelly.

"She's going through a phase," said Allie.

It was Allie who asked Mrs Kneebone if she would like to come to a meeting to form a steering committee for the Clare Street Community Project.

"Your help would be invaluable to us," she told her.

"Oh," said Mrs Kneebone, who was cooking a batch of pumpkin scones, the nearest recipe to carrot cake she could find. In fact, this was Mrs Kneebone's first attempt at baking since her Alec had died. Allie, coming to the back door and walking in like Mrs Towns, had taken her by surprise.

"Come on in," she called to Allie.

Allie came in and sat down. "Don't let me interrupt you."

Mrs Kneebone felt nervous with Allie watching her. She put the scones in the oven and sat down to talk. Allie told her all about the Clare Street Community Project, which was to be based on self-help between the inhabitants of the street and the surrounding area. Mrs Kneebone thought it was a good idea.

To Mrs Kneebone's delight the scones turned out light and fluffy. She set them out on the kitchen table with butter and jam, then sat down with Allie to eat them. She was getting used to sitting at the kitchen table with visitors, although it still didn't seem quite respectable. Respectability had always meant a lot to Mrs Kneebone.

"They're beaut scones," said Allie, spreading them with great dollops of butter and jam.

Mrs Kneebone felt very pleased. She thought maybe it was better to feel pleased than respectable.

Allie explained that a lot of changes were going on in and around Clare Street,. "We're not against changes," she said, "but we want to make sure that it's all done properly and nobody gets disadvantaged."

Mrs Kneebone agreed that it was very important that nobody should be disadvantaged. "But what changes do you mean?"

"Well, with these new, trendy people coming in, doing up old houses and redeveloping, there'll be a lot of changes. Prices'll go up. Rates'll go up. All costs'll go up."

"I hadn't thought of that." Mrs Kneebone looked worried.

"It's time everybody thought about it," said Allie. "We don't want the essential nature of the place changed, and we don't want people living here on pensions or welfare payments to have to get out, do we?"

Mrs Kneebone was looking alarmed. "We wouldn't have to get out, would we?"

"Not if we can help it," said Allie. "That's why we're forming this self-help group, so that old and new residents can work together to help one another."

"I'll do anything I can," promised Mrs Kneebone.

"Good!" said Allie. "Fred Towns and me have got together and organised a meeting."

"Isn't Mrs Towns one of the trendy people?"

"Yes, but she's all right. She wants to keep the *character* of the area."

"Well, if you think she's all right." But Mrs Kneebone was doubtful.

"She suggested that you should be on the steering committee. We need the help and advice of old residents," said Allie.

"Oh!" Mrs Kneebone was quite overcome, much too overcome to refuse. "If you really think I can help."

Later, when her natural timidity and caution had reasserted themselves she began to have some misgivings. If changes were coming should she have anything to do with them? She began to feel fear: the rock to which her life had been anchored seemed to be dissolving.

"Maybe you'd like to come with me," she said to Kelly. "Just to back me up."

"But I won't be able to go into the meeting," said Kelly.

"But you could come with me, anyway," urged Mrs Kneebone. "Just for the walk."

They walked down Clare Street and around the corner to Allie's house together. At the door of the room where the meeting was to be held, Mrs Kneebone was greeted by Mrs Towns, who gushed: "Oh, I'm so glad you could come! You're just the sort of person we need!"

Kelly went through the hall to the kitchen. Allie was there, trying to find enough clean, uncracked cups for the women at the meeting.

"Can I help?" asked Kelly.

Allie turned to her gratefully. "Oh, would you? I wouldn't bother, but Fed Towns turns up with the inevitable carrot cake, plus cream-cheese-and-celery sandwiches, and says everybody talks better over a cuppa. Don't know why we didn't have the ruddy meeting at her place! 'Specially since she's chairperson."

At that moment Fred Towns called from the other room: "Allie! We're ready when you are!"

"Go on," said Kelly. "I'll do this. Do you want tea or coffee?"

"Coffee, I reckon," said Allie, tucking her brightly striped shirt into her orange pants. "And thanks, kid!" She charged off into the meeting room, looking, Fred Towns said to Timothy later, like the *Rainbow Warrior*.

Kelly filled the electric kettle and switched it on. She found sugar and instant coffee in a cupboard and milk in the fridge. The fridge door was covered with stickers: *The Earth Needs Friends, Trees Mean Life, Together We Can Stop The Bomb, People For Nuclear Disarmament*. A big sticker on the oven door said, *This Is A Nuclear Free Zone*. Kelly put the coffee and plates of food on a trolley and pushed it into the meeting-room. She saw Mrs Kneebone sitting deep in a sagging armchair, looking dazed and sheepish. Like a dazed sheep, thought Kelly, giving the old woman a bright grin. Taking a cup of coffee and a piece of cake for herself, she went out onto the verandah. Sitting on the edge, swinging her legs over a garden of weeds and geraniums, she watched Allie's cat stalking birds and butterflies. With the children away at school it was quiet and sunny in the garden this early afternoon. From time to time Kelly could hear the conversation drifting from the meeting through the open window.

Fred and Allie seemed to be doing most of the talking. Mrs Towns was dressed in tight jeans and shirt, a yellow ribbon with the word *Shalom* on it and a *Women For Peace* badge pinned over her breast. Fred had ideas for fund raising: white elephant stalls, sales of arts and crafts, raffles, street stalls.

Allie wanted to have a community *drop-in* centre where the *different elements* of the local society could meet and help one another. "A place where you could get advice, attend classes on crafts and cooking and social awareness."

"Who would use it?" asked Helen Hopper.

Allie wondered who had invited *her*. "Everybody," she said, "from old age pensioners to young unemployed."

That hardly included *everybody*, though Helen Hopper, pulling her hand-knitted, hand-spun wool sweater neatly over her well-tailored skirt.

"It's a good idea," said Barbara Penton, a part-time welfare worker. "But you'd need a trained staff if you were going to offer advice."

"I've been giving advice all my life and I've never had any training," said Allie.

"That can lead to problems," said Barbara, thinking of Allie's own problems: her ex-husband and *those kids*.

Katie, a very young woman who had arrived with a child in a back-pack, which she left on the floor, wanted to know what they were going to do about Peace and the Environment. "And what about Aboriginal land rights?" she asked.

But nobody knew of any Aborigines living in Clare

39

Street with claim to any land there, so they didn't bother with that question.

"Natter, natter, natter," Kelly muttered to herself.

By this time she was getting tired of listening, so she jumped off the verandah and went round to the back of the house. She sat on a homemade swing tied to a branch of a big plum tree, and waited for the meeting to end.

When it did she walked home with Mrs Kneebone, carrying a rose bush in a pot. Mrs Kneebone said it was a *Peace* rose. The single flower had ivory-coloured petals blushing at the centre.

"Isn't it lovely? Allie gave it to me."

Helen Hopper had brought the rose to the meeting as some sort of gesture which only she understood. Allie had made a point of presenting it to Mrs Kneebone. Allie didn't like the Hoppers. She thought they were snobs, and, worse than that, Lionel Hopper was a real-estate shark. Allie thought he was probably out to get his hands on as much of the Clare Street area as he could, at the cheapest prices.

As they turned into Clare Street, Kelly saw a man and a boy in front of Mrs Kneebone's place. They looked as if they were just leaving the house.

"Who's that?" asked Mrs Kneebone.

"Looks like Mick and his dad," said Kelly.

The man hurried away when he saw them approaching, but Mick waited for them.

"Who was that?" said Kelly, looking after the man.

"Just me dad," said Mick.

"What was he doing here?"

"Nothin'."

"Why aren't you at school?" asked Mrs Kneebone.

"It's after school," said Mick. "I'm just goin' home."

"Come in, then," invited Mrs Kneebone. "Have some biscuits and cordial."

"Thanks," said Mick, "but I've gotta get home. Me mum said I wasn't t'be late."

"Oh well, you must do as your mother tells you."

Kelly watched Mick departing down the street. "I've never known him to turn down biscuits and cordial before."

"Maybe he's not feeling well," said Mrs Kneebone.

"He must be dying," said Kelly.

They went down by the side of the house to the back door. Mrs Kneebone always went in that way. This day she noticed the side gate was open. "I don't remember leaving that open," she said. She was usually very careful about shutting gates.

"Maybe someone else left it open," suggested Kelly.

"Who would do that?" Mrs Kneebone shook her head. "No, I just think I'm getting forgetful in my old age."

She opened the back door and they went inside. It was then she noticed that the back window was open. "Oh dear!" she said. "I must have been in a fluster when I left. I was so nervous about going to that meeting. Silly of me, wasn't it? Everyone was so nice."

Kelly was sure the back window and side gate were closed when they left, but she didn't say anything: she didn't want to worry Mrs Kneebone.

41

6

Something was missing, thought Kelly: something from the kitchen dresser. At first she couldn't think what it was, but she noticed a lack of balance in the arrangement of things. There was a space that should have been filled by something. Then she knew what it was: she remembered a little vase with painted fruit on a soft pastel background. She wasn't sure if Mrs Kneebone had noticed. The old woman didn't say anything about it, and she was a bit short-sighted. Maybe, thought Kelly, she could get it back for her before she noticed it was missing.

"I'm going to see Mick," she said.

Mick denied knowing anything about the disappearance.

"But you'd been in the house," Kelly insisted.

Mick shrugged. "What if I had?"

"You went in with your dad," Kelly accused him.

"So what?"

Mick stuck out his chin, and that was a mistake, because Kelly punched it. She had caught him at the back of Allie's house behind the raspberry canes. Now she threatened to drag him through the prickly things if he didn't tell her the truth.

"We didn't touch nothin'!" wailed Mick. "We just hadda look!"

"You pinched a vase," said Kelly. "And if you don't get it back I'll go the police about it."

"Ya wouldn't do that!"

"Don't bet on it!"

"Anyway, me dad's got it."

"But you're going to get it back."

"I can't!"

"You'd better!"

"I can't! Anyway, ya can't prove nothin'."

"I don't have to prove anything," said Kelly. "I just have to spread you all over Clare Street, you little squirt, if you don't get it back."

"All I can do is try," said Mick.

"You'd better try real hard!" warned Kelly. "Or else get yourself a new set of teeth."

Kelly waited for Mrs Kneebone to mention the missing vase, but the old woman said nothing, although she had noticed the space on the kitchen dresser. She noticed other spaces, too, of which Kelly was unaware, in the china cabinet in the lounge-room. The old woman, however, wasn't sure just what, if anything, was missing. She was getting so forgetful, she must have mislaid those things somehow, she thought. Kelly watched her dusting her china more often and thoroughly than usual, and counting her silver as she polished it. Why didn't she say something?

The truth was, for the first time in her life, Mrs Kneebone was beginning to speculate on the value of the contents of her little house. She realised she would have to make arrangements about the future: when she was dead. What would happen to her house and all her things? Now was the time to take an inventory, make arrangements. Everything would have to be left to someone *afterwards*. She had no relations. Who would want or need her things? What about Kelly? What about the Clare Street Community Project? The things she had could be of benefit to someone, she thought. As she looked ahead, Mrs Kneebone's view of life became both narrowed and expanded.

Kelly wasn't thinking about the future. She was too busy experiencing the present, with one experience getting lost in another. She didn't pause to consider the prospects ahead: next year, or the next fifty years. If she looked ahead at all she saw only a black hole in Space, a vortex of unknowable possibilities and disasters. Her only aim was to get the little vase back for Mrs Kneebone soon. Kelly's only future was *soon*.

But Kelly did not get the vase back. Mick said he couldn't get it. Sometimes he denied that he had anything to do with stealing it, at other times he said he didn't know what his dad had done with it. Kelly thought about going to see Allie about the whole thing. But what could Allie do? She had Katie on her hands at the moment. Katie, the woman who had come to the meeting with the baby in the back-pack, was staying with Allie, making placards and organising some kind of protest. She talked incessantly.

"People think people like me march and wave placards because we enjoy it," she told Kelly. "They don't care what we're demonstrating for."

Well, if they don't care, thought Kelly, why do it?

"People have to be made to think," said Katie. "They have to be changed. There have to be changes in people's thinking, their values, their ways of living. Power has to change hands. People have to have the power."

When that was done, she said, everything else would change, even climates, disturbances in the earth's behaviour from stress on the world's surface. Mrs Kneebone said there was a lot in what Katie said.

"We should all love each other," said Katie, "and love the world we live on. We should live for pleasure and the joy of living and not just for work, money and consumerism. Progress is just a rip-off!"

Katie wore T-shirts with Peace slogans on them, but there wasn't much peace where Katie was, thought Kelly. Even Allie got fed up with Katie, and said, "I wish you'd shut up sometimes."

"What do you want?" Katie would say to Allie. "I mean . . . in your life, what do you want? Most of all? Isn't it just to be a woman, strong and independent and in control of your own life?"

"Exactly!" Allie would say. "Now will you just shut up and leave me in control for a while!"

Kelly could see that it wasn't really the right time to try to talk to Allie about Mick or his dad.

A few days after the theft, however, Kelly was sure she saw the vase in Timothy Towns' antique shop. She went in and looked at it closely. Yes, it must be Mrs Kneebone's vase. Timothy came up to her. "You're Kelly, aren't you?" He was very tall, and stood over her, looking down at her.

"Yeh," she said, looking up.

"Like that vase, do you?"

"Yeh," said Kelly again.

"You've got good taste," said Timothy approvingly.

"Where'd you get it?" asked Kelly

Timothy cleared his throat. "A local gentleman."

"How much is it?"

"I think the price is marked on it."

Kelly looked at the small tag. Thirty-five dollars! She drew in her breath. "Wow!"

"That's not expensive. It's signed, as you can see," Timothy explained. "Very good value, really."

"Could I put it on lay-by?" asked Kelly. "Pay a bit now and the rest later."

"We don't do that usually," Timothy began, then looked at Kelly's eager face. "But as we're neighbours . . . "

"I've got some money," said Kelly quickly. "I can give you four dollars to start with if you could put it away until I can pay it off."

Timothy hesitated.

"I want it as a present for Mrs Kneebone."

"Oh, I see!" Timothy smiled. "Well, I expect she'll be delighted. And in that case I'm sure I can hold it at least for a short time." He turned to the old man who had just entered the shop from out the back somewhere. "What do you think, Mr Ryan?"

The old man came forward, and stood quite close to Kelly. She thought she could smell whisky.

"What do I think of what?"

"This vase."

"It's beautiful."

"But do you think we should put it away on lay-by for this young lady?"

"I can put down four dollars," said Kelly. She still had most of the money Peg had tucked into her sleeping-bag before she left, and could go up to six dollars if they insisted on more.

Old Ryan looked at her closely. "Haven't I seen you somewhere before?"

"Me?" Kelly backed away a few paces. She hoped the old man wouldn't remember the day she had run from the shop with Peg, knocking over some ornaments as they went. He might want her to pay for the breakages.

Timothy had taken Kelly's four dollars and was making out a receipt. Although he had asked for it, he was clearly not interested in the old man's opinion. You could tell who was in charge of the business.

"Keep that," he said, handing the receipt to Kelly. "Bring it with you when you come to make other payments."

"Thanks." Kelly took the receipt and folded it carefully.

Old Ryan was still looking at her closely. "You live around here, do you?"

"Yes," said Kelly.

"She lives with old Mrs Kneebone," said Timothy.

"Oh, Mrs Kneebone!"

Watching him, Kelly saw the old man's attention shift suddenly.

"Haven't seen her for ages. Thought she must have gone away." He looked at Kelly again, but this time he clearly wasn't thinking of her. "Remember me to Mrs Kneebone. Tell her Pat Ryan was asking about her."

"Yes, I'll do that." Kelly was moving away. Old Ryan followed her.

"Tell her I remember her Alec. Poor old Alec!"

"Yes, I'll tell her."

Kelly was already on her way down the street. Old Ryan turned back into the shop. As she hurried away Kelly heard him whistling a tune. As she turned the corner she found herself singing the words of the tune to herself:

> When you walk in the valley alone,
> You will hear my lonely cry.
> Far from beyond the land of dreams,
> As the lonely summers go by.

7

At the opportunity shop the following Thursday, Mrs Swann remarked on how Mrs Kneebone had changed. "You look as if you're blooming," she said.

Looking in the mirror, Mrs Kneebone saw that her face was certainly very red. She was feeling light-headed, almost girlish. She hoped it wasn't her blood-pressure. "I've had a very busy week," she said. "But I have enjoyed it." She told Mrs Swann all about the visits she had had from Fred Towns and Allie Jones, and Allie's children, and about the meeting of the steering committee of the Clare Street Community Project.

"We call it the Clare Street Project," she explained, "but it's really for the area all around Clare Street."

"Then why call it the Clare Street Project?" asked Mrs Swann, thinking that her street ought to have been included.

"Well," explained Mrs Kneebone, "we could hardly call it the Clare Street-Willis Street-Park Street-Flinders Street-Mary Street-Main Road Project. Clare Street is the one street intersecting all the others."

"Anyway," said Mrs Swann, changing the subject, "how is that little orphan of yours?"

"Kelly!" exclaimed Mrs Kneebone. "Such a pleasure. She's a nice little girl, and very musical. We've been singing round my old piano in the evening."

Mrs Swann felt a sudden pang of jealousy. She tried to imagine Mrs Kneebone in this cosy scene at the piano in her lounge-room. Instead, she saw in her mind's eye her own teenage grandchildren, waiting, bored, for the visit to Grandma to come to an end. They were like strangers now, fidgety, disdainful, so *knowing* in their manner they made her feel nervous. She could remember — such a short time ago it seemed — when they were Nanna's darlings, so natural and innocent. But now they seemed cool and aloof, shrugging off affection, evading questions. They were like silent strangers in ugly clothing and artificial hair-styles. She had heard, indirectly, that Josh, the eldest, was on drugs. Surely that couldn't be true. Not her Josh! In desperation she had said to him, "Josh, don't you believe in God any more?"

"Knock it off, Gran!" he had said, looking embarrassed. "Nobody believes in God any more, not even God!"

Now Mrs Swann drew in her breath, and told Mrs Kneebone about this, blinking back tears. "Wasn't that a terrible thing to say?"

Mrs Kneebone patted her old friend's shoulder. "Yes," she said, "but he probably didn't mean it. They try to shock you at that age, you know."

Mrs Swann shook her head. She couldn't see how Mrs Kneebone could understand children at any age. "But it was a terrible thing to say! A terrible thing to believe!"

"Sad, too, when you think about it," said Mrs Kneebone. She felt sorry for Mrs Swann, and sorry for Mrs Swann's grandchildren. "It's the future and all the uncertainties ahead of them."

"Well, who was ever certain about the future?" asked Mrs Swann. "We weren't were we?"

"No," agreed Mrs Kneebone, "we weren't. But perhaps they *are* or think they are. They don't believe in any future, not for them, not with the unemployment and the bomb and all that." Mrs Kneebone was thinking of Katie, who said there had to be changes in people's thinking and values and ways of living. "All we can do," she said, "is love each other and the world we live on."

"But I do!" cried Mrs Swann. "And I love my grand-children!"

"I know, I know," said Mrs Kneebone. "And I'm sure they love you." She looked at Mrs Swann, and loved her, realising it was something she had not thought about before. At that moment she would have embraced her old friend if she had not been sure that such a spon-taneous act of love would have startled, confused and embarrassed her. At the same moment, Mrs Kneebone felt a great surge of affection for everyone, for her own little world of Clare Street, for Allie and Fred, for Katie, the children, and even for Helen Hopper, but most of all for Kelly. At the same time she was afraid for the fragility of that small world, and all the other small worlds of animals and plants upon the whole perilous Earth. She could have wept then at her own view of a lonely, frigh-tened planet with a magnitude of dangers threatening it. Then she saw that Mrs Swann still had tears in her eyes. She pressed her old friend's hand.

"I'll make us a cup of tea."

Kelly had a job at a coffee shop. She had to make money somehow to pay for Mrs Kneebone's vase. She went to Allie for advice, and Allie said she ought to be getting the dole. Katie, who was listening, asked her, "D'you want a part-time job?"

"Anything," said Kelly.

"Well, there might be a lunch-time job at this coffee shop," said Katie.

It was Helen Hopper, suddenly public-spirited since the Clare Street Project meeting, who had asked Katie if she would like the job. The coffee shop belonged to a friend of the Hoppers.

"Five dollars an hour," said Katie. "I told her it would cost more than that for a baby-sitter."

But five dollars an hour sounded like a fortune to Kelly. Katie wrote out the address for her, and said, "You'd better hurry if you want it. And tell them you're a friend of Helen Hopper's."

Kelly arrived in the middle of a busy lunch hour, and the rushed owner of the shop asked her if she could start right away. Kelly worked hard, doing her best to make a good impression, clearing tables, washing up and stacking dishes, making pots of tea and coffee, and occasionally toasting raisin-bread or sandwiches. At two o'clock in the afternoon the owner said, "You've only been here for an hour today, so that'll be only five dollars." But she said she wanted Kelly to work for two hours a day, including Saturday, but not Sunday, from twelve noon until two in the afternoon.

"That will be ten dollars a day, paid each Saturday."

Kelly couldn't believe her good luck. At this rate she would be able to get the vase back for Mrs Kneebone by the end of the week. Her second day at the shop, which was Thursday, the day Mrs Kneebone was at the opportunity shop, Kelly worked hard and cheerfully, and stayed on after two o'clock, washing and stacking dishes. The owner was very pleased with her. She thought of giving her extra money for the extra time, but decided instead to give her a slightly damaged chocolate-cream sponge cake, which she put in a box for her. Kelly carried the cake home, knowing how Mrs Kneebone would enjoy it.

Mrs Kneebone had had a busy day. The opportunity shop had been crowded. On top of that she had suffered one or two dizzy spells. Mrs Swann was worried about her and wanted her to go home early.

"But I couldn't leave you by yourself," said Mrs Kneebone. "Not when we're so busy."

When Edna Crabbe came in just after two o'clock, Mrs Swann told Mrs Crabbe that she thought Mrs Kneebone wasn't well.

Edna Crabbe looked at Mrs Kneebone. "You do look flushed, dear. Maybe you're getting the flu. There's a lot of it about."

Mrs Kneebone said there was always a lot of something about, and she couldn't leave Mrs Swann on her own.

"That's all right," said Mrs Crabbe. "I'll stay."

So the two women prevailed upon Mrs Kneebone to go home early. If they hadn't, things might not have turned out so tragically.

To tell the truth, Mrs Kneebone had to admit that she wasn't feeling too well. On her way home she began to feel better and stopped to look in the bakery window. She decided to get some cheese-and-bacon rolls and an apple-pie for tea. At the shop on the corner of Clare Street she bought cream for the pie. When she arrived home the first thing she noticed was that she had left the back window open again.

"Oh dear!" she thought. "I am getting so forgetful. I'd lose my head if it wasn't screwed on."

Kelly passed the antique shop on her way home. Timothy Towns was carrying a box of old books from his car, and she stopped to talk to him.

"I'll be able to pay for that vase in a couple of days."

"I might have something else in here you'd like," said

Timothy. "On the other hand, Mrs Kneebone must have a lot of nice stuff in her place. You don't know if she'd like to sell any, do you?"

"I don't reckon" said Kelly. "It's all old family stuff. She'd have more room to move, though, if she got rid of some of it."

"Why are you buying her some more, then?"

"It's to replace something . . . something she lost."

"Lost?" Timothy frowned. "How did she lose it?"

"I'm not sure," said Kelly. "If I was sure I'd . . ."

But she didn't say what she'd do, she just shrugged her shoulders and walked on. Old Ryan came out and watched her until she turned the corner.

"That girl reminds me of someone," he said. "I wish I could remember."

Still fretting about her forgetfulness, Mrs Kneebone had opened the back door of her house and entered the kitchen. She put her shopping bag on the table, then turned to the open window.

"Fancy leaving it like that," she said to herself. "You silly old goose!"

Then she noticed the dirt on the window ledge and on the side of the sink. She looked closer at it. It looked like garden soil. At that moment Mrs Kneebone heard a sound behind her: a movement, quick and threatening. An icy tingling of fear, starting at the base of her neck, seemed to snap-freeze her. She wasn't able to move or make a sound. The threat moved closer, came up behind her, exploded in her head. She fell sideways into darkness.

When Kelly arrived about ten minutes later, the first thing she noticed was the open door; then she saw Mrs

Kneebone lying motionless on the kitchen floor with a stain of blood under her head. Her first impulse was to run away. Panic almost blotted out every other instinct. She had to hold herself back, to force herself not to run but to bend over the old woman and feel for her heartbeat and listen for her breathing. At least she wasn't dead. But what could Kelly do? Panic kept swelling up inside her, telling her she would somehow be held responsible. They would say it was her fault. Police would come. She would have to answer questions. Who was she? What was she doing here? Why hadn't she reported the theft of the vase? Why was she trying to buy it back? Panic urged her to run. *Now*. They would find her guilty. Guilty! *Guilty*. She had no rights. No mother. She couldn't even prove her own identity. Who was she, anyway?

Kelly had to tell herself what to do. "Stop! Think! Call an ambulance."

She had dropped the chocolate cake on the floor, and now she walked over it as she rushed to the telephone. With trembling, fumbling fingers she dialled the emergency number.

"Send an ambulance," she shouted in response to the voice of inquiry at the other end of the line. "An old woman. Attacked. Injured. Clare Street."

She gave the house number, repeated it, repeated the name of the street, the name of Mrs Kneebone. All the time she was staring across the hall into the quiet, chintzy room Mrs Kneebone had given her. The possessions she had brought from Allie's place were there, rolled up in her sleeping-bag, lying against the wall as if waiting for this moment of departure. The waterproof cape was folded on top of the sleeping-bag.

Kelly had gone when the ambulance arrived. She did not go out the front door or along Clare Street. She

threw her few possessions over the back fence and followed them into the garden behind, knowing that the
couple who lived there would be out at work. She ran
through their garden into the next street, hesitated, and
turned right. She did not know where she was going. She
did not know how long she had walked when a man in a
truck offered her a lift. When he said he was going
somewhere north or north-east, she said that was where
she was going. In the middle of all her panic and horror
and desperation she felt calm, like the eye of the storm.
She wondered if death felt like that.

8

Kelly had no clear idea of where she was or where she was going — or even *why* she was going. When the man who had given her a lift stopped his truck and said, "This is as far as I go," the day had turned to evening. The sun was well down in the west. Kelly turned east, walking quickly away from the town into open country. Sea and sand lay to her left and sloping paddocks to her right. There was very little traffic on this quiet, narrow country road, running through dune and farmland to distant isolated beaches and national parks. Kelly made no attempt to thumb her way now. A few cars passed, but nobody offered her a lift.

She began to work out what could have happened to Mrs Kneebone. The old woman had been mugged, for certain! But why? Who would do that? Robbery, Kelly decided, that was why. And Mick's dad, for sure, had done it. He must have been in the house when Mrs Kneebone surprised him. He had attacked her; not to kill her (he wouldn't do that, would he?) but to give himself a chance to get away. He had probably crept up behind her. Maybe she hadn't even seen him, couldn't say for sure what had happened. And who would suspect Mick's dad? Only Kelly. It seemed as though she had played right into his hands by not telling anyone about her earlier suspicions. Especially now that she had run away. What a fool she had been to run away! But if she hadn't there would have been so many questions to answer. She hated questions. "Never answer any questions," Peg always said. Peg never answered questions. Not even Kelly's questions.

By the time she found a place to sleep, Kelly was so weary, so worn out, she opened her sleeping-bag and crawled into it at once. It seemed as if the whole world had curled away from the sun into a little ball of dark shadow. She had found an old shed in a paddock, and spread out the sleeping-bag on top of her waterproof cape. She placed her pack under her head and closed her eyes, but did not fall asleep right away. She tossed and turned.

"You fool!" she murmured, wearily but angrily. "Fool! Fool! Fool!"

Why had she run away? She was not responsible for what had happened. But a voice in her head said, "*Yes, you were.*" Because she had not wanted to alarm Mrs Kneebone, and because Allie was always too busy to listen, she had not told anyone about her suspicions. And now, by running away, she had completely damned herself. She had acted as if she had been guilty. Oh, why had she been such a fool?

When she fell asleep at last, she was troubled by bad dreams. She sat up in the darkness, crying out: "Aunt Fanny! Aunt Fanny!" She thought she was a little girl again, and her mother, Peg, was running away with her in her arms. Peg was saying over and over again, "Forget it! Don't talk about it! Don't ask or even think about it. It's not *our* fault, it's *their* fault."

Behind them, a big woman, who had been shouting

57

and screaming a few moments before was lying as still as death at the bottom of the steps. Another woman — *Gramma* — was watching them go, her hands pressed to her face in distress.

"Gramma!" Kelly cried out in her sleep. "Gramma! Gramma!"

Shaking off her nightmare at last, she lay trembling. "Peg," she whispered. "Peg, what happened?"

But there was nobody there to answer. The question had always been there, but never an answer. What had they been running away from? Why were they always running away? Peg had taken Kelly right away from Tasmania, right to the north of the mainland to a place called Mullum, where they had lived outside the town with a group of people Peg called 'the family', although Kelly knew they were not *her* family. Peg would never talk about her own family.

"Just forget that lot!" she would say. "They'll do us no good!" They were better off in Mullum, she said, finding a new way of life for themselves through creativity and self-development. And it was good there for a while. Kelly liked it, and they had stayed a year before running away again. Kelly remembered there had been an argument about some lost or stolen property or something. It had always been like that: periods of peace in one community or another, then trouble again, accusations, arguments which did not always involve them but always ended in their running away. After Mullum they had come south gradually, until eventually they had arrived right back in Tasmania. But they had never seen Gramma again, or Gramma's family.

"Forget them!" said Peg.

She would not speak of them, and so, gradually, Kelly had seemed to have forgotten too. Now the memory troubled her with some other thought of violence, some other, forgotten fear, as she stared into the darkness.

She fell asleep again, but fitfully. From time to time she heard scuffling sounds in the shed, and the wind gusting in the loose iron roof. Once she opened her eyes and looked into the round face of the moon. It was nearly full and seemed so close she could almost count its scars and craters. When the first streaky light of day was visible in the sky she crawled out of her sleeping-bag and rolled it up carefully. She saw that except for a few bales of hay, the shed where she had spent the night was almost empty. In spite of the early coolness she felt hot and thirsty. She went outside to look for water. There was an old tank on a broken stand at the side of the shed. Although it was rusty and holey, surprisingly clear water flowed from the tap. Kelly drank from her cupped hands, and splashed water over her face and hair. She looked up and saw a golden glow spreading over the eastern hills.

Going back into the shed she found a couple of sacks behind the bales of straw. She opened one and looked inside. The sack was half-filled with shrivelled, sprouting potatoes. She looked into the other sack, and found old, yellow Golden Delicious apples. A lot of these were nearly as shrivelled as the potatoes, but Kelly was hungry. She picked one out and bit into it. It was soft but not bad. She ate it all and selected another one.

As she was eating she wandered round the shed and discovered an old bicycle in a dark corner, covered with dust and cobwebs and old sacking. Dragging it out into the light, she examined it carefully, rubbing it down with some sacking. She saw that it had a bit of rust on it, but otherwise seemed in a good condition, with sound wheels and tyres. She tried it out, riding it round the shed and testing the brakes. This was just what she needed, she thought. She was not thinking about *stealing* it, just about *needing* it. If she had a bicycle she would not have to ask anyone for a lift, she could manage on her own. At least until she found Peg. She had decided that she definitely *must* find Peg, that somehow Peg would be able to explain why she had run away, and why they were always running.

After she had neatly stowed her scant belongings in her pack, filling it with the best of the apples from the sack, Kelly rolled her sleeping-bag in the waterproof cape and secured everything to the bicycle with a piece of old rope she found under the tank stand. Then she set off. At that hour of the morning the rough road was free of traffic, so she kept going straight on with no idea where she would find Peg.

9

Mrs Kneebone was feeling very strange. She was lying in hospital with a bandage round her head and her arm in a sling. Her head ached, and when she opened her eyes everything seemed unbearably bright. She thought she could hear someone talking, but the voice seemed a long way away. Painfully she turned her head to one side and saw a stretch of polished floor between her bed and the wall. On a bedside cupboard she saw a vase of flowers. Slowly and carefully she turned her head the other way and saw that the bed beside her was empty. Closing her eyes again she gave a long, trembling sigh. A feeling of sadness descended upon her; it seemed as if ice had settled around her heart. *Something terrible had happened.* For a moment Mrs Kneebone gave herself up to self-pity. Tears began to trickle from her eyes. Then she sniffed impatiently, wiped her eyes on the edge of the sheet, and blinked rapidly to clear them.

"Don't be such an old fool!" she told herself, sharply.

"So, you're awake, are you?"

The voice came from across the ward. Mrs Kneebone peered through a kind of mist which seemed to be hanging over the room. She saw that there were four other

61

beds in the mist, and one of them, in the far corner, seemed to be occupied.

"Are we the only ones here?" she asked.

"Yes, in this ward," said the occupant of the other bed. Mrs Kneebone could faintly make out a large, grey-haired woman. "But of course this is just for us oldies. Soon as they can they get rid of us to the geriatric place down the way."

"Oh," said Mrs Kneebone. "Do they?" She wondered what had happened to her glasses.

The other woman sat up in bed. "Been in an accident, have you?"

"A sort of accident," said Mrs Kneebone. She felt dizzy from trying to peer across the room and closed her eyes again.

She could faintly remember that she had been conscious when the ambulance had arrived, with Fred Towns following just behind.

"When I saw it stopping here," Fred had said, "I thought I'd better come along to see what had happened and if I could do anything."

To Mrs Kneebone it had seemed as if the kitchen and everything in it were floating round her head.

"Where's Kelly?" asked Fred.

Kelly was not there. Mrs Kneebone wanted to tell Fred Towns that Kelly hadn't been there, but her mouth trembled when she tried to speak.

"She must be here," said Fred. "I saw her go past my place."

Mrs Kneebone shook her head until the pain of movement blinded her and she thought she was going to be sick. The ambulance man said, "Now, now, love, just take it easy."

"Well, who phoned for the ambulance?" asked Fred.

The ambulance man shrugged.

62

"*Somebody* must have," insisted Fred.

The ambulance woman tucked a blanket round Mrs Kneebone. "Don't you worry about anything, love," she said. "We'll soon have you safely in hospital."

Mrs Kneebone had tried to thank her, but she could feel consciousness slipping away from her, and was glad to let it go.

A nurse came into the ward, brisk and smiling. "How are you, dear?" she asked.

"All right, thanks," said Mrs Kneebone weakly. She would have liked to ask some questions, but she hadn't the strength, and was not sure that she wanted to know the answers.

"Do you feel like having visitors?" asked the nurse.

"Who?" asked Mrs Kneebone, but before the question was answered Fred Towns was through the door, with Allie Jones behind her.

"We thought you'd need some things," said Fred. She opened the drawer in the bedside cupboard and began filling it with garments and other things out of a bag she had brought with her. "I've just brought a couple of nighties, some soap and talcum powder, things like that." She closed the drawer, and smiled at Mrs Kneebone. "There you are! We'll get your own things for you if you want them, later on."

"Thanks," whispered Mrs Kneebone. She was wondering who the things belonged to — the things Fred had put in her drawer.

"I borrowed them," said Fred, in response to the unasked question. She patted Mrs Kneebone's hand reassuringly. "They're quite respectable."

Allie was standing beside the bed with a brown paper-bag in her hands. "I've brought some grapes and apples," she said, looking round for a bowl.

"Have you got anything to put them in, dear?" Fred asked Mrs Kneebone.

"I don't think so," said the old woman. She lifted her head to look for the nurse, who had gone.

"You'd better go and find something, Allie," said Fred. She noticed that the grapes were making holes in the bag.

"Okay, I'll see what I can find," said Allie, going out into the corridor.

Fred found a chair on the other side of the ward. She brought it over and placed it beside Mrs Kneebone's bed. She sat down after glancing at the other patient in the ward, who was lying back with her eyes closed as if asleep. Leaning forward, Fred said to Mrs Kneebone, very softly, "You don't know where Kelly is, do you?"

Mrs Kneebone answered with only a very slight shake of her head.

"Nobody's seen her," said Fred. "Not since the . . . the *accident*."

Mrs Kneebone said nothing. She closed her eyes.

"But, as I told you at the time," said Fred, "I'm sure I saw her going past my place. Just after you went past."

"*After*?" Mrs Kneebone felt that she had to get that straight. "Did you say . . . after?" Her eyes were wide open now.

"Yes, *after*. And just before the ambulance came. It must have been Kelly who phoned for the ambulance.

"No, " said Mrs Kneebone. "Kelly wasn't there."

"She must have been," insisted Fred. "I saw her go past my place after you went past."

Mrs Kneebone shook her head, and a sharp pain stabbed her between her eyes.

"Are you all right?" asked Fred, anxiously.

"Yes," said Mrs Kneebone, but avoided nodding her head again.

"How did you do it?" asked Fred.

"Me?" said Mrs Kneebone.

"How did you hit your head?" asked Fred. "You must have fallen over." She wondered if Mrs Kneebone could understand what she was saying. "Did you fall against the table? Or the dresser?"

Mrs Kneebone said nothing.

"Don't you remember?"

"No."

"Did you see Kelly?"

"No."

But Mrs Kneebone remembered she *had* seen Kelly, just for a moment, as she floated in and out of consciousness on the kitchen floor. Remembering that Kelly had been there raised questions that Mrs Kneebone didn't think she wanted answered.

Fred Towns explained again how she had been painting the veranda and had seen Kelly go past. "I saw everybody who went past."

"Who else did you see?"

"Nobody. Just you and Kelly and then the ambulance."

"You're sure?"

"Nobody I recognised."

"Anybody you didn't recognise?"

"Why?" said Fred. "Was there someone else?"

"I don't know," Mrs Kneebone said helplessly, "I don't know."

"There, there," said Fred, patting the old woman's hand. "Don't you worry about it. There's always a simple explanation for everything."

Mrs Kneebone was so confused at that moment that she doubted there could ever be a simple explanation for anything.

Allie returned at last with a plastic bowl. "Got it! It was a battle, but I won!" She waved the bowl triumphantly in the air. Then she put it on the bedside cupboard and emptied the fruit into it. "That nurse!" she said, exasperated. "You wouldn't believe it! She was so reluctant to hand over this ruddy plastic dish, with a crack in it incidently, you'd have thought it was Waterford glass!" Having arranged the fruit, she leaned over Mrs Kneebone. "Keep you eye on that nurse," she warned. "Mind she doesn't nick your fruit!"

Mrs Kneebone smiled faintly.

Allie sat down on the end of the bed. "How are they looking after you?"

"Very well."

"You don't look too good."

"I'm all right."

"No problems?"

"No, none."

"Good!" Allie stood up. "Well, if everything's all right I think it's time we were going.

"Already?" said Fred.

"We don't want to tire Mrs Kneebone out, do we? She needs her rest."

"Oh, yes. Of course," said Fred. Before she stood up she wrote something on a piece of paper and slipped it into the drawer. "That's my phone number. Get the nurse to ring up if you need anything."

"Thanks. You're very kind."

"Well, I always say, what's the use of neighbours if they can't do anything for you?"

"We'll be in to see you again," said Allie.

"Thanks," said Mrs Kneebone again.

"Keep your eye on that nurse," advised Allie before she left.

"And don't worry about anything," said Fred. "See you tomorrow!"

As they were leaving the hospital, crossing the car-park, Allie said to Fred, "Well, what do you think?"

"She can't remember anything," said Fred. "Couldn't even tell me how she fell, or where she hit her head, or anything."

"Did she say anything about Kelly?"

"Not really."

"Odd, isn't it? The kid disappearing like that."

"I wonder why. Do you think she had anything to do with what happened?"

"No." Allie brushed the idea aside with a movement of her hand. "Kelly's a good kid. Though I reckon she'd have a bit of a temper at times."

"Why do you think she's disappeared?"

"Damned if I know. Shock, maybe," suggested Allie. "Mind you," she added, "she's not the sort of kid you'd expect to stay anywhere for long. Not if she's like her mother."

"Mother? Isn't she supposed to be an orphan?"

"She might as well be," said Allie. "Peg's no use to her."

"Why?"

"She's a bit of a ratbag. Got lost in the Flower-Power era and doesn't know where she is today."

"Kelly seemed fairly sensible to me," said Fred. "That's why I think it's so strange that she disappeared." She fished in her handbag for her car keys. "I think we should do something."

"About what?"

"About Kelly."

"But we don't know where she is."

"That's what we ought to find out." Fred started her car and pulled out of the carpark. "Supposing Mrs Knee-bone didn't fall? Supposing she was hit on the head?"

"By Kelly, you mean?"

"By someone."

"Who?"

67

"I don't know, but as soon as I saw her, the first thought that came into my mind was that she'd been mugged."

"*She* hasn't said that."

"She says she can't remember."

Allie stared at Fred, wide-eyed. "You're not suggesting that Kelly did it? She wouldn't!"

"What I mean," said Fred, patiently, "is that Kelly might have *seen* something, and that's why she's disappeared. Maybe we ought to talk to the police."

"But aren't they supposed to investigate why an ambulance is called out?"

"Are they?" said Fred. "But even if they did, and they find an old woman has fallen in her kitchen and hit her head, what's there to investigate?" Fred shook her head. "I think we ought to contact them."

Allie thought about it for a moment. "Well, at least we could report Kelly as a missing person."

Kelly pedalled fiercely, straining to drive the bicycle uphill and then freewheeling down, through avenues of pines, of sheoaks, and then boobyallas. Sheep were grazing in paddocks that curved gently into the dunes on one side of the road and up to the low hills on the other. Ahead lay a saw-edged line of low mountains. Kelly had no idea where she was going. The landscape seemed empty of people and towns. The few farmhouses she passed could have been uninhabited for all she knew. She saw nobody. She pedalled faster and faster, the wind flapping her clothes and making her eyes water. The faster she went the greater was her sense of release, of escape from something too big to cope with. She did not want to remember anything, to think about anything. She only wanted to ride on and away, faster and faster. Unconscious of the pain in her legs and back, she concentrated on driving herself on, without any plan or in any particular direction. She did not know how long or how far she had travelled when she stopped at a roadside shop to buy a loaf of bread and a small carton of milk. She spent most of her small supply of money on these items. She drank the milk at once, but knew that for the next few days she would have to live on the bread and the apples she had taken from the shed.

The one thought in Kelly's mind was that she had to find Peg. The reasons in her life for moving on or running away were always tied up with Peg. What was the secret she did not understand, that Peg would never explain? Was she guilty of something? What? She couldn't remember. But if questions were asked about her, what would be discovered? She had to find Peg. Only Peg knew the answers.

She found another shed in which to spend the night. It was small and warm. Sheltered by bales of straw she fell into a deep sleep. She slept soundly for several hours, until she was awakened suddenly by the noise of a car engine, and men shouting outside. There was a bright light somewhere; it swung across the shed, shone into her eyes for a moment, than passed on. Kelly flung herself out of her sleeping-bag and ran to hide behind the open door of the shed. The light moved away with the roar of a moving truck. Looking out, she saw the truck swaying up the hill and two men standing on the back with a bright light, shining it over the top of the driver's cabin. They had rifles. As the truck bumped over the ridge of the paddock, she thought she saw a fleeing figure for a moment against the skyline. The guns blazed, the figure disappeared. The men shouted as the truck dipped down over the ridge and was lost from her view, although she could still see the glow of the swerving light.

Hunters!

Kelly was afraid. The men with the guns had sounded rough and menacing. She began to roll up her things, preparing to run away again. She had already tied everything to her bicycle when she heard the men and the truck returning. The truck stopped. Kelly held her breath. The men were arguing with one another.

"Get on with it! Try the other paddock."

"What about a drink first?"

"There's none left."

"Waddaya mean, none left? Didn't we 'ave a case o' tinnies?"

"We finished 'em."

"All of 'em?"

"You been sittin' drinkin' while we've been doin' the work?"

"Ya think drivin's not workin'?"

"Orright! I'll drive! You get up 'ere!"

After more arguing the men drove off again. Kelly listened as the truck disappeared into the distance. As soon as it had gone she jumped on her bicycle and pedalled wildly over the paddock and the cattle grid, out onto the road and away into the night.

She travelled along the middle of the road, always looking over her shoulder to make sure the truck was not following. The road narrowed into a track and finally reached a crossroad. Kelly hesitated, wondering which way to go. She decided to take the wider road, lined with bushes where she could hide if the truck followed her. Again she was driven by the unreasonable belief that there was safety in movement. Her life with Peg had been lived on the move: like a migratory bird, she could see that she was not meant for a permanent nest in Clare Street or anywhere else. She had spent years with Peg, moving over the surface of life, following the music, the experiences, the meaningful relationships of the next (after the last) encounter, gathering and scattering the days.

Clare Street was not for her, she thought bitterly. Something had caught her there; not just Mrs Kneebone and her friends, but something else. It was not just the idea of a settled life, but something she couldn't name, that filled her with such sadness now that she had lost it.

10

Mr Ryan was working at the back of the shop fixing an old gramophone. Timothy Towns was sorting books and pricing them. The younger man was looking worried about something, old Ryan thought.

"How's Mrs Kneebone?"

"She's still in hospital," Timothy replied.

"Nasty sort of accident, that," said Mr Ryan.

Timothy stacked the books as he priced them. "It's funny about the kid."

"Kelly?" said the old man. "She didn't come back to get that vase, did she?"

"No, though she said she'd be back. I saw her the day of the accident."

Ryan couldn't find out what was wrong with the gramophone. "I'll go and make some coffee."

He wasn't really needed here, the old man thought as he made the coffee. He ought to move out, get away into the country somewhere. He was useless in the shop, but he would be just as useless in the country. If only he had somebody he could make plans with, do things with. He should have a grandchild somewhere, he thought. But where? The child would be a big boy now; sixteen or seventeen. Ryan always thought of the child as a boy, just like his son, Patrick.

Timothy took his mug of coffee and stood in the open doorway of the shop, gazing along the street. He saw the new police sergeant, Jack Green, approaching.

"G'day, Jack."

"G'day, Tim. How's business?"

"Pretty quiet."

There was nobody else in the street. The sergeant stopped to talk. "Nice weather, nice long summer," he observed.

"There's something I ought to talk to you about," said Timothy. "Can you come in for a minute?"

"Sure."

Jack followed Timothy into the shop. "Trouble, is it?"

"Maybe," said Timothy.

The two men sat on the edge of a table, looking out through the doorway.

"You know that Mrs Kneebone," said Timothy, "the old lady who had the accident?"

"I know."

"She had a kid with her, Kelly. The kid's missing."

"I know she was staying with Mrs Kneebone, but I don't believe that was her home, nor that the old lady was her legal guardian. The kid hasn't been reported missing from home."

"But she hasn't been seen since the accident. Don't you think that's strange?"

The sergeant shrugged. "Kids go missing every day."

"But I saw Kelly on the day of the accident," said Timothy. "Probably just before it happened. She was buying a present from me for the old lady and said she'd pick it up next day. She was buying a vase."

"And she hasn't collected?"

Timothy shook his head.

"What vase?" asked the sergeant.

Timothy showed the policeman the little vase he had put aside for Kelly.

"Is it worth much?"

"About thirty-five dollars," said Timothy. "But that's not the point. My wife says Mrs Kneebone *had* a vase exactly like this one. She saw it on her kitchen dresser. But next time she looked, she says, it wasn't there."

"Where did you get it?"

"From a man who comes in sometimes. He knows good stuff. I've bought a few things from him."

"What things?"

"Some I've sold," said Timothy. "But I put the rest away. In here." He opened a cabinet and took out some of the ornaments and other things he had bought from Terry Jones. "I have no reason to believe that he didn't come by them honestly."

The sergeant examined the objects. "Then why are you telling me about them?"

"I've got this *feeling*," said Timothy.

The sergeant looked at him sharply.

"That they might have something to do with Mrs Kneebone."

"No theft has been reported. Nothing reported missing."

"There's another thing," said Timothy. "Terry Jones seems to be missing as well. I tried to find him to ask him about this stuff. I know where he lives, but he wasn't there. I've tried the place several times, but as far as I can find out he hasn't been seen there since . . . since the accident."

The sergeant picked up one of the objects on the table, and studied it for a moment. "You haven't asked Mrs Kneebone about any of these things?"

"I thought maybe you should ask her," said Timothy.

The sergeant put down the object he was studying. "You'll have to come down to the station and make the inquiry official, first."

Timothy called out to old Mr Ryan, asking him to keep an eye on the shop for a while.

"By the way," said the sergeant as they walked down the street together, "your wife came in to see me earlier. She had a few questions to ask me as well."

When Mick arrived home from school that afternoon his mother was talking on the telephone.

"Why should I think it's funny that *he's* disappeared at the same time as Kelly?" She looked over her shoulder, and saw Mick standing there, listening. Somehow he knew Allie was talking about his father. "Okay, Bigears! Get out of your school clothes and get washed."

Mick did not move. Allie turned her attention to the phone again. "Look! What are you suggesting? That he had something to do with Mrs Kneebone's accident and Kelly's disappearance? What do you think he is? Well, I know he's violent at times, but that's personal. He's not indiscriminate about it. As for the police, they can ask me anything they like. I'll tell them when they ask!" Allie slammed down the phone. "The nerve of some people!" She saw Mick still standing there. "Do as I told you!"

"What's Dad done?"

"Nothing! Go and get washed!"

Mick changed his clothes, and stood in the bathroom letting the water run over his hands. His dad had only pinched a few things, he thought, he wouldn't do anything bad. After splashing his face, he went into the kitchen. Mandy was there spreading bread with peanut butter.

"What do you think's happened?" he asked.

"Wotcha mean?"

"Dad's gone."

"Good riddance!"

Mick opened the packet of sliced bread. "Do you think Mrs Kneebone really fell down and hit her head?

Mandy spread honey over the peanut butter. "No, I bet that Kelly bashed her on the head and ran off with all her money."

"You're stupid!" Mick grabbed the peanut-butter jar.

"I bet she had a fortune," said Mandy. "Saved it up all her life."

"She'd have it in the bank though, wouldn't she?"

"Old people don't trust banks. They keep their money in tins under their mattresses."

"Who could sleep on a mattress with a tin under it?"

"Maybe she buried it in the garden."

"You're mad!"

"So are you!"

Mick made a chocolate drink by pouring topping into a glass of milk. Allie came into the kitchen.

"Do you kids know if your dad ever went to Mrs Kneebone's place?"

Mick did not answer. With her mouth filled with peanut butter and honey sandwich, Mandy said, "He never even knew her, did he?"

"Don't talk with your mouth full," said Allie.

"Then you shouldn't ask me questions when I'm eating," said Mandy.

Mick stirred his chocolate and milk with his finger, and said nothing.

11

A bridge crossed a narrow gorge where the road curved into town. The river filled a little rock pool beside the picnic park. Kelly passed it and rode on into town. Dirty and hungry, she pushed her bicycle along the main street. It was an old town. Most of its buildings probably dated from the last century and had been recently restored with an eye to the tourist industry. There was a pub, a general store, a post-office, even an 'Olde Hot Bread Shoppe' among the markets, arts-and-crafts and antique shops. Kelly counted the money in her pocket: a dollar and forty-five cents. She looked into the window of the hot bread shop. What would she buy? She had almost decided on a large bacon-and-cheese bread roll for fifty cents when she saw stale buns for sale at twenty cents each.

"They're only yesterdays," said the woman behind the counter, looking at Kelly with distaste. One of those unwashed greenie's kids, she was thinking. There were too many of them coming through the town. Kelly bought two buns, and started eating before she was out of the shop.

As she pushed her bicycle along the main street she ate the buns quickly and hungrily. A police car with two policemen in it passed her and pulled in at the pub ahead. One policeman got out and went into the pub, and the other one sat in the car watching Kelly approaching. As she came nearer he opened the door of the car and got out. She thought he was going to speak to her, but at the same moment the other policeman came out of the pub and called out to him. With one more glance at Kelly he followed his colleague into the pub. Kelly jumped onto her bike and rode quickly out of town.

She began to look for somewhere secluded, a creek or river where she could bathe and wash her clothes. The late summer sun was continually disappearing behind clouds although no rain fell. Just before midday she came to a picnic area beside a caravan park. She saw a red-brick building with a sign in front: WOMEN. It was a toilet and washroom. Leaving her bicycle hidden behind a tree beside a small caravan, Kelly took some clothes from her pack and walked casually over to the building. The door was locked. She should have expected that. As she was wondering what to do she looked over her shoulder and saw a man standing in a doorway marked OFFICE. She thought he was watching her. She began to move away, then a woman opened the door and tried to come out with a heavy washing-basket in her hands. Kelly rushed forward to hold the door open for her.

"Thanks," said the woman.

As soon as the woman was through the doorway, Kelly slipped inside, closing the door behind her.

To one side of the door she saw rows of toilets, and on the other side shower-rooms and washbasins, with a couple of washing machines right at the end. In one shower she found a small used bar of soap. The water was wonderfully hot. Kelly soaped and scrubbed herself and washed her hair. She even washed her dirty clothing under the shower, and put on fresh clothes. She had to dry herself with a T-shirt because she had no towel, so her hair was wet when she left the building, and her skin was slightly damp under her clothes. She had wrapped the soap in a piece of toilet paper and put it into the pocket of her jeans.

As she stepped outside again she saw the man still standing in the doorway of the office. Calmly she walked towards the clothesline as if she had a right to be there. A few pegs had been left on the line and she used these to hang up her washing. She decided she would wait in the picnic area and give her clothes time to dry out a bit. She had returned to her bicycle, and was about to move away when the door of the little caravan beside her opened and a small, grey-haired woman looked out.

"Oh, is that yours?" she said. "I wondered where it had come from."

"I've been looking for someone," said Kelly quickly.

"Who?" asked the woman. "I know nearly everybody here. We've been here all summer."

"The Ryans," said Kelly. Her own name was the first one she thought of.

"Ryans?" The woman frowned in thought. Then "Oh, the Ryans!" she cried. "Yes! They were here, but I'm afraid they've gone, dear. Left a couple of days ago."

Good, thought Kelly, but she said, "Oh dear, that's too bad."

"Yes, it's a pity you missed them. Have you come far?"

"Far enough on a bike," said Kelly. She was feeling tired from her journey and almost sleepless nights.

"You look as if you could do with a cuppa," said the woman.

Kelly was wary. "I must be going." She was turning away when she saw the man from the office. He was walking down the road towards them. "On second thoughts, I'd love a cuppa!" she said quickly, and followed the woman into the caravan.

A grey-haired man was arranging plates of bread, cheese and tomatoes on the table.

"This is my husband," said the woman. "Our name's Beattie."

"I'm Kelly Ryan."

"*What*?" Mr Beattie seemed to be deaf.

"Ryan," repeated Mrs Beattie, loudly. "You know? They were staying here, behind us. Went home a couple of days ago."

"Weren't they the Reillys?" asked Mr Beattie.

"No. *Ryan*." The woman appealed to Kelly. "That's the name, isn't it?"

"Yes," said Kelly, avoiding Mr Beattie's eyes.

Mrs Beattie turned to her husband. "This little girl came on her bike, you know. Such a long way. We can't let her go on without something inside her, can we?" She turned back to Kelly again. "What would we tell the Ryans if we saw them again?"

"The name was Reilly," insisted Mr Beattie. Still looking at Kelly, he said, "Have you come far?"

"From Launceston," she answered. She wished she hadn't come in. She didn't like the way Mr Beattie was looking at her. She didn't like being questioned.

"Come on! Sit down! Eat up!" Mrs Beattie encouraged her. "We know what an appetite young people have, don't we, Dad? We've got children and grandchildren." She told Kelly that she and her husband were retired now and travelling around Australia in their caravan.

"Did you ride from Launceston in one day?" Mr Beattie asked Kelly as his wife paused for breath. "On a bike?"

"No, I stayed somewhere on the way."

80

"A bit young to be running round by yourself, aren't you? Shouldn't you be at school?"

"I'm sixteen."

"You don't look it. Anyway, what's sixteen! Should still be a school kid. Where's your parents?"

"My father's dead."

Mrs Beattie was instantly sympathetic. "Oh! you poor little thing! Have a bit of cheese."

"What about your mother?" asked Mr Beattie.

"I'm going to . . . " Kelly began. She was about to say she was going to *find* Peg. She stopped herself, and said, "I'm going to my mother now."

"Why haven't you been with your mother?"

"John! It's none of your business!" admonished Mrs Beattie.

"I've been staying with a friend," said Kelly.

"What sort of friend?"

"An old lady." Kelly wanted to get away. She did not want to answer any more questions. "I've gotta go!" She pushed herself back from the table.

"Now look what you've done!" Mrs Beattie turned to her husband.

"I was just *asking*," he said.

"You were interfering," declared Mrs Beattie. "Once a policeman, always a policeman! It sounded like a cross-examination."

"Just interested," said Mr Beattie mildly.

Kelly was standing up. "I really do have to go."

"That's all right, dear," said Mrs Beattie. "But finish your tea. Have something more to eat."

"I've had enough, thanks."

"But you'll get hungry riding your bike all that way," declared Mrs Beattie. She began to wrap up bread and cheese, while Kelly waited impatiently, and Mr Beattie told her, "You'll never make it back to Launceston to-night."

81

"I know," said Kelly, "but I've got a place to stay."

"Where?"

"With my . . . my grandmother."

"That'll be nice for your grandmother," said Mrs Beattie.

She waved goodbye as Kelly rode away, calling after her, "Give my regards to the Ryans!"

"The name was Reilly," said Mr Beattie.

An hour later, Kelly remembered her washing on the line back at the caravan park. Well, she thought, she wasn't going back for it. She had stopped to rest, sitting under a tree by the side of the road. She ate a piece of cheese and wondered what she was going to do now. She couldn't just go on and on without any idea of where she was going or why, or where she could find Peg. She only knew there were questions about herself that had to be answered. Looking back on her life, she could see that she and Peg were always running from questions about themselves. But now she *had* to find the answers. And this wasn't the way, she thought. She could have been travelling in circles for all she knew. She was no nearer to finding Peg, no nearer to having the questions answered. She had to think. Where would Peg go? To places where they had been before? To friends they had known? No, Peg never went back, she always went on.

And there was also the question of Mrs Kneebone. Kelly did not think she had been really badly injured, but she didn't know for sure. She would have to find out, because whatever had happened to Mrs Kneebone, directly or indirectly, had been her fault. And what would the old woman think of her running away? If only she could explain! But she couldn't explain until she understood. At least she could ring up someone and find out about Mrs Kneebone, she thought. But who? Was there anyone who wouldn't start asking her more questions if she phoned them? Mick? Yes, she could handle Mick, she decided. But — how could she be sure of getting Mick on the phone? Probably Allie or Katie or someone else would answer it. Well, she would just have to try. She had a dollar coin in her pocket; she decided she would get it changed into ten cent coins and make the phone call.

As she was pedalling towards the next town in search of a telephone box, she was passed by a van with the name of a theatre company on its side. Strange faces appeared at the windows: one long-nosed and narrow, others furry and catlike or doglike. Strange voices called out to her: *Yoo-hoo! Squibs-and-Crackers! Barnacle! Cockalorum! White-Famed Simminy! Pondalorum!* Kelly almost fell off the bicycle in surprise. Hands waved to her and she waved back, laughing, as the van disappeared round a bend in the road ahead.

What on earth was that? she said to herself. Another question, she thought, as she pedalled on in search of a telephone.

12

That morning the Jones's cat was found dead; run over by a car right in front of Allie's house. It was the same little cat which Kelly had watched stalking birds and butterflies in Allie's front garden on the day of the meeting of the steering committiee of the Clare Street Community Project. It was known simply as 'the cat' to everyone except Mick. He called it 'Piddles' because that is what it did, everywhere. And that was why it was always shooed out of the house. "Get that cat out of here!" they would shout, usually at Mick, although it had been given to Mandy as a kitten, and afterwards lived in the garden in trees and high places, leaping from its perches to come and curl round Mick's legs, purring, when he arrived home from school.

Now that it was dead, thought Mick, he was the only one who cared. Today everyone else was busy getting ready for the peace rally. Katie was finishing posters and blowing up balloons. His mother had typed out leaflets with peace songs on them. Mandy was busy making a hat and cloak, covered with badges and ribbons. It was mad, thought Mick. He wasn't going to any stupid peace rally. If it made everybody too busy to care about a dead cat, what was the use of it?

When the telephone rang, Allie called out, "Mick! Answer that, will you! You're the only one not doing anything!"

Mick *was* doing something. He was making a coffin out of a shoebox. But he got up and answered the telephone, which was fortunate for Kelly. If Mick didn't answer, she had decided, she would disguise her voice and ask for him. If anyone sounded suspicious she would hang up. So she was very relieved to hear Mick's voice at the other end of the line.

"Mick! Listen! It's Kelly here. Don't let anyone else know I'm ringing!"

"Waddaya want?"

"I want to know about Mrs Kneebone. How is she?"

"Orright."

"Where is she?"

"In hospital. Where are you? Everybody's been askin'."

"But they don't think I had anything to do with what happened, do they?" asked Kelly.

"I dunno."

"Well, *I* didn't! And I think you know who did, don't you?"

"Why should I?"

"What did Mrs Kneebone say about what happened?"

"Nothin'. She doesn't remember."

That worried Kelly — Mrs Kneebone not being able to remember. "Are you sure she's okay?"

"Yeh. They reckon she can go home in a coupla days," said Mick. "Anyway," he asked, "Why didja run away?"

"I don't know. I was stupid. I'll try to explain when I get back."

"Yar comin' back?"

"Of course I am. Soon as I can. I have to find Peg first. But I want you to let Mrs Kneebone know I phoned.

Will you tell her, Mick? Only Mrs Kneebone, nobody else."

"Orright."

"And you're sure she's all right, aren't you, Mick?"

"Sure!" said Mick. Then he asked, "Didja know Josh's run away too?"

"Josh?"

"Mrs Swann's grandson. I reckon she's a bit suspicious about you an' Josh disappearin' at the same time."

"I don't even know him!"

The red light was flashing. Kelly pushed in another twenty cent coin. "Listen, Mick! I'll have to hang up in a minute. Be sure you tell Mrs Kneebone I called. Tell her I'll see her as soon as I can."

"Yeh, okay," said Mick, and then he remembered to tell her about the cat. "Piddles is dead."

"Who?"

"The cat."

"Listen, Mick, I have to go," said Kelly. "Tell Mrs Kneebone!"

She didn't care about the dead cat either, thought Mick. "Aw, piss off!" he said. He hung up.

"Who was that on the phone?" asked Allie.

"Nobody," said Mick.

Katie looked at him sharply. "Aren't you getting ready for the rally?"

"I'm not goin'."

Katie stood over him, hands on her hips.

"What do you mean *not going*? Who do you think we're doing this for? We're doing it for kids like you, so that you can have some kind of future ahead of you."

Mandy joined in the attack. "You're stupid, Mick! Don't ya wanna stop the big powers from makin' bombs and attackin' everybody?"

Mick shrugged. He knew it was no use pointing out

that he hadn't even figured out how to stop *Mandy* from attacking *him*. "What's the use?"

"What's the use," mimicked Katie. "That's a fine attitude! That's a typically *male* attitude!" She rounded on Allie. "Do you encourage your son to take an attitude like that?"

Allie sighed. "Have you got the balloons ready yet?" she asked.

"Balloons!" shrieked Katie. "It's *attitudes* I'm talking about! If we can't change attitudes in the home, where can we change them?"

"If we want to have peace," said Allie, "let's start in the home. Right now! No coercion! Mick knows what we think, but he's entitled to do what he wants. *Right*?" She looked at Mick. "What are you going to do?"

"I'm going to see Mrs Kneebone," Mick said.

"Well, that's nice," Allie approved. "You can take the washing I've done for her."

"Her washing?" said Katie. "I thought Fred Towns was doing that."

"The day Fred Towns keeps her mouth shut and actually does something," said Allie, "that'll be the day!" She was tired. She stretched her back and looked at the mess of balloons, paper, scraps of material, badges and other stuff all over the room. She moaned. "All that junk!"

Mick could see that they had forgotten about him. He had lined the coffin-shoebox with soft material, and now he took it outside and put in sprigs of herbs. On top of these he placed the dead cat. Then he dug a hole and buried it under the rosemary bush. After he had done all that, he felt as though there was something else he ought to have done. He thought about it for a moment, then he began to sing:

*"O come all ye faithful, joyful and triumphant,
O come ye, O come ye, to Beth-le-hem."*

After she had made the phone call to Mick, Kelly was
far from reassured about Mrs Kneebone. Should she go
back? And if she did go back, what good would it do?
No, she thought, she would go on, find Peg. But she
must plan things out properly from now on. She would
have to try to think of all the places where Peg might go.

As she pedalled out through the town she noticed that
the bicycle had a bit of a wobble. She hoped it wasn't going to fall apart. She stopped when she came to a little
park by the side of the road. She saw that the theatre
van that had passed her had stopped there. Two young
women and two young men were sitting on the grass.

"Hi!" said one of the young men.

"Hi!" said Kelly. She moved away and took out her
sandwiches.

"Come and eat with us," the other young man called
out to her.

"Yes," said a blonde young woman. "Have some coffee
with us."

"Thanks." Kelly moved over to join them. The taller
young man stood up and said, "Let me introduce everyone. This is Becky, Emma and Evan. Collectively we are
the Playground Puppet Theatre." He bowed, and added,
"My name is Chris. We perform in playgrounds, market
places, backyards, street malls, at fairs, anywhere when
the weather's fine."

"I'm pleased to meet you," said Kelly.

Emma handed her a plastic cup of coffee. "What's
your name?"

"Kelly. Kelly Ryan."

"Help yourself to cake."

"I've eaten a lot today," said Kelly. She had already finished the bread and cheese Mrs Beattie had given her.

When Chris asked Kelly where she was going, she replied, without thinking, that she was going looking for her mother.

"Where did you lose her?"

"*How* did you lose her?"

"Weren't you being rather careless?"

Kelly laughed. "I didn't lose her!" But it was difficult to explain about Peg to anyone who didn't know her. And maybe she had *lost* her. Maybe she would never see her again. "I've been staying with friends," she said.

"And where has your mother been?"

"Oh . . . Peg moves about a lot."

"Like us?" asked Chris. "Is she 'in the theatre' as we jokingly say?"

"She's a singer."

"What's her name?"

"Peg. Peg Ryan."

"Peggy Ryan! Hey! We saw her last week." Chris snapped his fingers to trigger his memory. "Where was it?"

"In Hobart," said Emma, "with the Carmondy Country Folk."

"Sure!" said Chris. "Con Carmondy's group. Not exactly a swinging name, but it's a good group. It's been going well for years. But now it's *sensational*. Wow! Your mum's made all the difference!"

"And they're in Hobart?" asked Kelly.

"They were last week. That's when we saw them. But I reckon they'll be off to the mainland any day now. They're good!"

Emma looked at Kelly. "Didn't you know?"

Kelly shook her head. Her heart sank. Would Peg go

away to the mainland again without letting her know?

"What about you?" asked Chris. "Do you sing like your mother?"

"No, not like Peg."

"Hey!" again Chris snapped his fingers. "Was your father Paddy Ryan?"

"Yes, he was."

"I wondered when I saw Peg if she was one of the old *Peepee* Ryan duo," said Chris. "Peggy and Paddy Ryan. I saw them when I was at high school. They sang at an anti-war rally in Melbourne."

"I don't remember my father," said Kelly.

Chris remembered one of the songs Peepee Ryan sang at the Melbourne anti-war rally. He began to sing:

> *"I would lend a hand to my brother,*
> *I would give my heart to my lover,*
> *But I would never a soldier be,*
> *No, no, never, not me!"*

"I can't remember all the words," he said, "but it had a good catchy tune. The kids liked it. I remember at the end we all sang together:

> *"We would never be your enemy!*
> *No! No! Never, not we!"*

"My father was a pacifist," said Kelly.

"Some said he was a draft-dodger," remembered Chris. "But people always say things like that. Anyway, he was very popular in those days. Peepee Ryan was a very popular duo."

"What about you, Kelly?" asked Becky. "Have you ever sung on the stage?"

Kelly shook her head. Then she laughed. "No, no," she sang, "Never, not me!"

Emma and Evan had two large puppets beside them — a very shaggy dog and cat. When Kelly saw them she said, "They're two of those funny things I saw hanging out of the window of your van when you passed me on the road."

"*Funny things*!"

"Did you say 'things'?"

The dog puppet jumped up. "I'm a Doxy-Doodle! That's what I am, a Doxy-Doodle!"

The cat puppet leapt onto Kelly's leg. "What do you mean by *thing*? Can't you see what I am? I'm a White-Faced Simminy!"

The two puppets began to dance around Kelly.

"I'm a Doxy-Doodle!"

"I'm a White-Faced Simminy!"

"Doxy-Doodle! Foxy-Poodle!"

"White-Faced Simminy! Soot-Faced Chiminy!"

Kelly laughed.

"Watch out! Mind the water bottle!" cried Chris.

But it was too late; the bottle had been knocked over, and the water was trickling into the grass. Leaping about wildly, the puppets, Doxy-Doodle and White-Faced Simminy, were shouting: "The *Pondalorum*! Look! We've spilled the Pondalorum!"

Chris picked up the water bottle. "Come on!" he said. "It's time we were on the road again. We've got a performance tonight, remember."

The puppeteers jumped up at once. "Yes, yes, Master of All Masters!" They began to clear up the coffee cups and other things, throwing rubbish into the bin. In throwing out the last of his coffee, Evan splashed Becky's jeans.

"Mind my Squibs-and-Crackers!" she shouted at him.

Kelly looked on in amazement.

"You think we're crazy, don't you?" said Emma. "In this sort of work it helps to be crazy."

"Helps?" cried Chris. "It's absolutely *essential*!" He

had opened the back of the van. Turning to Kelly, he said, "I suppose you'll be going to Hobart to find your mother. If you're mad enough to come with us, we can give you a lift at least part of the way."

Kelly said she was mad enough, and they all crowded into the van, and somehow managed to squeeze the bicycle in as well.

The puppeteers were only going as far as the next town, where they were giving a performance that evening in the CWA hall, and another performance at a big street fair the following morning.

"Sunday morning," said Emma.

Was it only Saturday? To Kelly it seemed such a long time since she had left Mrs Kneebone's house on Thursday afternoon. But if she could find Peg quickly in Hobart, she thought, and discover why it was that they were always running away, she would be able to go back and explain things to Mrs Kneebone very soon. While she was thinking she picked up a very strange puppet dressed in a tight jacket and baggy trousers fastened round his thin legs below the knees. He had long, thin feet in black shoes, and a long, narrow face with a long, thin, bent nose and very large eyes.

"My better half," said Chris. "I am he, and he is me." He began to explain the story of their play. It was based on an English fairy tale, he said, about a funny old gentleman who liked to be called 'Master of all Masters'. He lived all alone with a cat and a dog, and he gave very uncommon names to very common things. He had no wife and no family, and one day he decided he was tired of looking after himself. So he hired a servant girl, and tried to teach her all the extraordinary names he used for ordinary everyday things.

Suddenly all the puppets seemed to jump up and start talking to one another.

"He calls himself Master of All Masters!"

"More like Misery of all Miseries!"

"He calls me White-Faced Simminy."

"What? Soot-Faced Chiminy?"

The dog puppet popped up behind Kelly' shoulder. "He calls me Doxy-Doodle! But you can call me any time, Kiddo!"

Kelly laughed.

"You're the audience," Becky told her. "You have to help the servant girl to remember the silly words."

Then all the puppets seemed to begin talking at once.

"House? It's not a house! It's a High-Topper-Mountain!"

"Did you say Fly-Paper Fountain?"

"The Master's trousers are Squibs-and-Crackers!"

"What? Fibs-and-Quackers?"

"No! No! Spits-and-Smackers!"

"Fire is Cockalorum!"

"Pop-on-morum?"

"Cockadoodle!"

"Water is Pondalorum!"

"Pour some more on!"

"It's all *Pandemonium*!" cried Chris.

And it was indeed, thought Kelly.

Time and the journey passed very quickly with everyone joining in the game of the play. Taking her cue from the puppeteers, Kelly shouted out the names with them. The more everybody shouted the more mixed up the words became. When Chris explained that in the last part of the play where the house caught fire after the Master of all Masters had gone to bed (which he did not call a bed but a 'barnacle') everything became even more confusing.

"Master of all Masters! High-Topper-Mountain is on fire!"

93

"Cockalorum has broken out!"

All this caused a great hullabaloo to break out in the van. Passing motorists turned and stared.

"Fire! Cockalorum! Cockalorum!"

"Wake up, Master of all Masters!"

"Get up out of your Barnacle, put on your Squibs-and-Crackers!"

"Get the Pondalorum to put out the Cockalorum before High-Topper-Mountain burns down!"

"Help Doxy-Doodle!"

"Help White-Faced Simminy!"

Words were mixed up. They cried out 'Cockadandle!' and 'get out of your Bonacle!' and 'put on your Fibs-and-Squackers', and 'Fly-Paper Fountain and Flapper Pumpkin is burning down!'

Kelly laughed until her sides ached. She was sorry when they came to the end of their journey.

"You can stay and watch the *real* performance if you like," said Chris.

Kelly said thanks, but she decided to go on. She wanted to get to Hobart as soon as she could. Chris lifted her bicycle out of the van. "I hope it holds together," he said. He looked at it dubiously. Kelly thought it would be all right, at least as far as Hobart. The puppeteers said goodbye. They were in a hurry now to prepare for their performance.

Kelly had started to ride away when Chris called her back. "Wait a minute!" He had taken a notebook out of his pocket and was writing something in it. Tearing the page out and handing it to Kelly, he said, "That address might find the Carmondy guy. It's his group your mother is with. If you go there they'll know where you can find him."

"Thanks!" Kelly read the address, then folded the

paper and put it in her pocket. "Thanks a lot!" Her luck had changed, she thought.

"So long, kid! And good luck!" Chris turned away. He went to help Evan lift the boxes out of the van.

As she rode away Kelly turned back once and waved. She thought she would like to be a puppeteer one day.

13

Mrs Kneebone was looking sadly at Mick. He had just told her about the death of Piddles.

"It seems to be a bad time for us, doesn't it?"

"It was really Mandy's cat," said Mick. "Only she didn't look after it. Now somebody's gone an' run over it."

"And now God has taken Piddles up to heaven," said Mrs Kneebone.

"Why?" asked Mick. "What would God want with a dead cat?"

Shocked by the question for a moment, Mrs Kneebone wondered, as Mick did, about the vagaries of the Almighty. She too had been puzzled these past few days. "Well," she said, "I don't suppose that God looks at things the way we do, or sees us just as you or me or a dead cat, and not very important. I suppose He must see something else, something we can't see."

"Our souls?" asked Mick tentatively.

"*Something*," said Mrs Kneebone, who wasn't really sure what it could be when she thought about it. "But whatever it is, He *cares* about it."

"Katie says," Mick told her, "that ya shouldn't say 'he'

when talkin' about God. She says God isn't a man."

"I suppose she's right," said Mrs Kneebone. "I don't suppose God is a man. We just think about God that way because we can't really imagine *God*. Any more than we can imagine what God sees in us, or in a little cat."

"D'ya really think God cares?"

"If you care, God must care so much more."

"Ya reckon? *I* wouldn't 've let Piddles get run over," declared Mick. "Not if I was God an' could 've stopped it."

Mrs Kneebone sighed. "You think God could have stopped it?"

"Why not? If he cared!"

"I'm sure He cares." Mrs Kneebone was quite convinced of the truth of her statement in spite of unsubstantial evidence to support it. She thought of the wars and cruelty and all the disasters happening in the world.

"Why are ya sure?" asked Mick. "Why does God let bad things happen?"

"Maybe He thinks that what we do is *our* responsibility. *We* should take more care and not run over little cats and other animals. Or do bad things."

"I didn't run over it!" said Mick.

"*Somebody* did," said Mrs Kneebone. "And the thing is — *everybody* has to care. If it's our world, it's our responsibility. God gave it to *us,* so *we* have to care."

"I do care," said Mick. "I cared about Piddles. But I couldn't get anybody else to care."

"Yes, that's the problem," said Mrs Kneebone. "Everybody has to care."

"It sure is!" agreed Mick. "There's some people who'd blow up the world 'n' everythin'!" He had suddenly decided he was going to the peace rally after all. "See ya later!" he said, and was almost out through the door when he remembered Kelly's phone call. Coming back into the ward, he said quickly, "Kelly rang up."

"Kelly?" Mrs Kneebone felt her heart jerk. "When?"

"This mornin'. Said to tell ya she'll be back soon."

Mick was heading for the door again when Mrs Kneebone called out, "Wait! Come here!"

"I've gotta hurry," said Mick, but he came back.

"What else did she say?"

Mick thought about it for a moment. "She said I wasn't to tell anybody, only you. She wanted to know if ya was orright, an' I said ya was."

"Did she say why she'd gone away?"

"Not really. Said she wants ta see her mum."

"*Her mum*. Why?"

"Didn't say. It was long distance. She didn't have much time. But she said ta tell ya she'd explain when she gets back." Mick was edging towards the door again.

"Who is her mum?" asked Mrs Kneebone.

"Peg is," said Mick. "She's mad! She went 'n' fergot Kelly!"

"What is she like?"

"Mad! I tol' ya!" Mick was at the door now. "I've gotta go! I'm goin' to a peace rally!"

"Yes, of course," said Mrs Kneebone. "Of course. Off you go! Don't miss the peace rally."

Kelly felt that her chance meeting with the Puppeteers had somehow changed her luck. She was excited and cheerful. She knew something important was about to happen to her. As she pedalled out through the edge of the town it seemed to her that everything was strangely familiar. It was not that she *recognised* anything, but she *knew* this place. She was certain of that. She could not name a single house or shop or street, yet she remembered it. It was like a dream memory passing through her mind. It seemed inevitable to her that she should be here, that she should have been brought to this place by that happy band of performers. There was some substance of the imagination at work. It was as if a play or film were unfolding and she had found herself onstage or in front of the camera.

When she came to a side road, not signposted, beyond the edge of the town, Kelly turned down it, pedalling under the wide-reaching arms of the trees growing along one side. On she went, on and on, along the endless curve of the road, round and round, dazzled by the evening sun, low in the sky. Although the road was rutted and cracked, with gravel spreading out loosely from either side, she allowed the bike to gain speed on the downhill run. She sped through the long shadows, singing, so certain was she that she was held for that moment in the hand of Fate. She crossed a narrow creek on a single-lane bridge. Its planks rattled. Suddenly she remembered a time when she was a very little girl and played with another little girl, brown-eyed and amber-skinned, with hair like dark honey. She looked at the scattered houses as she passed. When she came to a broken gate and saw the old wooden house at the end of the track, she stopped. *She knew that house.* She stood staring at it for a moment, then pushed her bike down the track. She was almost breathless with expectation.

A woman came out of the house and stood on the verandah, shading her eyes against the low, northern sun, watching Kelly approach. Yes, thought Kelly, *that was her*. A big dog pushed past the woman and ran to meet her, whining and barking and wagging its tail. Kelly bent down to pat it. The dog licked her face. The woman stepped down from the verandah and came forward.

"Who are you?"

"I'm Kelly!"

"Who?"

The woman came towards her, widening her dark eyes as if to take her in. The low sun placed long shadows between them.

"Kelly?"

The woman seemed uncertain. She came closer. "Why, bless my soul!"

"Gramma?" Now Kelly was uncertain. "Are you?"

The woman crossed the shadows and took her in her arms, hugging her as if she would smother her. "I always knew you'd come back! Come on! Come in!"

Gramma was a big woman, well-built, with short, grey curly hair and tawny skin. She pushed Kelly into a chair in the kitchen. "I always knew you'd come back some day."

"I didn't know," said Kelly, still surprised. "I found my way by accident."

"Accident or not, who knows the way things work? I've been wishing you back here since Peg took you away. You've been in my prayers every day."

Gramma made tea, the steam rising up round her face. She poured it out and pushed one of the big mugs across the table to Kelly. "After all," she said, "Tassie's not such a big place. When I heard you'd come back from the mainland I knew you'd get here sooner or later."

"But we got back ages ago, Gramma!"

Peg had come back to join the protest against the damming of the Franklin, and stayed here.

"Well, I said you'd be back sooner or later," said Gramma, "but you certainly took your time."

"Your mother was ashamed of us, and that's why she took you away."

The evening had turned chilly, and Gramma and Kelly were sitting on each side of the open fire, with the big dog lying between them.

"Was that the only reason she took me away?"

"Peg didn't need any other reason. It was all right to leave you here when you were little, I suppose, and not noticing such things. Anyway, she didn't have time for you then. She was a big success. Singing all over the place. Melbourne. Sydney. Up north. Everywhere. And I was glad to have you here. It wouldn't have done you any good being with Peg, dragged around the country with the weird sort of people she knew."

They sat and talked for a long time by the fire. Gramma asked Kelly about her life with Peg, and Kelly told as much as she could remember. She told Gramma how Peg had left her with Allie Jones, and then about Mrs Kneebone.

"She must be a nice woman, that Mrs Kneebone," said Gramma.

"She is. She's very nice."

Kelly did not tell Gramma why she had run away from Mrs Kneebone's house. She couldn't explain that, not even to herself. Aware of the girl's reluctance to speak of it, Gramma didn't ask. She only said, "Where are you going now?"

"I'm looking for Peg."

"I don't see why you should go looking for her. Not when she left you like that. Peg was never any good to anyone — least of all herself."

"But she is my mother."

"Yes. And I'm *her* mother," said Gramma. "But she'd rather forget that. She'd rather forget her own blood. She's ashamed. But we're proud of that blood."

"Is that the reason she left?" Kelly sounded doubtful.

"What other reason?" asked Gramma. "I told you, Peg was ashamed."

Kelly still felt doubtful. She thought there must be another reason. She bent down to pat the old dog. "Fancy Jason remembering me all those years."

"You're about the same age, you know. And you were great friends, you and Jason."

Smoothing down the dog's ears, Kelly said, "Gramma, what do you know about my father?"

"Nothing much. He was small, like you. But she never brought him here. I think he was just like her. *Wild*. They were both wild. But they were very young. Too young for sense. But some people never get sense, no matter how old they are."

"Was she very fond of him?"

"Mad about him! Oh, yes! Never cared about anyone or anything else in her life," said Gramma. "Just him and the music. Unless it was you," she added.

"What about you? Her own mother?"

"I told you, she was ashamed of me. Of all of us." Leaning forward, Gramma took another log out of the basket and put it on the fire. "It would make her mad when other kids called her half-caste. It's not nice to be called names, especially when you get *official* names like that." She leaned back in her chair again. "But I'd tell her, like I told all the kids, there's no cause to be ashamed of anything, not unless it's something *you've done*." She laughed softly. "When Peg would stand up to me and say, 'I've got more *white* blood in me! Look at me!' I'd just tell her straight that all blood is red. Not black or blue or any other colour. Just red."

Kelly laughed.

Gramma looked at her sharply. "She never told you, did she?"

"No."

"Well, I'm telling you now. And I can tell you who you are and where you came from, and who your ancestors

102

were. You can be proud of it because it's *real history*."

Kelly turned her eyes from the light of the leaping flames to the amber glow of Gramma's face. She felt warm and sleepy. "But what about Aunt Fanny?" she asked softly.

"Aunt Fanny?" For a long time Gramma gazed into the fire without saying any more. Finally she chuckled. "Aunt Fanny! So you remember her?"

"Sort of," said Kelly.

"She'd be hard to forget. Yes," said Gramma, "she'd be hard to forget. Fanny was a problem, I won't deny it. A fighting woman. And the drink didn't do her much good. But generous, and good-hearted in her own way. And she loved kids. Peg had no cause to hate her the way she did."

Kelly waited for Gramma to go on, but she sat silently gazing into the fire. "What happened to Aunt Fanny?"

Gramma stirred herself. "What happens to us all in the end? She's dead." She pushed herself out of her chair. "I'll get us another cuppa."

Gramma went into the kitchen, and Kelly sat and listened to the sounds of the tea being made. She didn't move. The old dog put its head on Kelly's knee and she stroked it absently.

"I'm not surprised," said Gramma, coming back with the tea tray, "that Peg didn't tell you anything."

"Did my father know?"

Gramma poured tea and handed a mug to Kelly. "I don't know. Peg never said anything, not if she could help it. And nobody could tell, not by looking at her, not unless they saw her with me or some of the family. It shows in some of us more than others. But it's not what *shows,* it's what you *know* that matters to you."

"But if Peg felt the way she did," said Kelly, "why did

103

she leave me with you instead of my father's mother when they went to the mainland?"

"With *her*!" Gramma exclaimed. "She *hated* her. They hated each other, I reckon. I think your father's mother blamed Peg for him giving up the university and taking up with music the way he did, then going away to the mainland. No, Peg wouldn't have anything to do with *her*, not with that woman. And I don't think that woman ever wanted to have anything to do with Peg either. There was a lot of bad feeling between them. Bitterness is a dreadful thing." She sighed. "I know some bad things happened to Peg," she said. "But a lot of it she brought on herself. She'd never face the truth. And for all she's my own daughter, I have to say she never did have any sense. She was a silly girl and grew up to be a silly woman. And that's the truth. Always wanting to be somebody else!"

Gramma told Kelly that when Peg realised that she had a good voice and that people liked to listen to her sing, she had her mind set on success and applause. "She had a good time while it lasted, but it was a terrible shock to her when it came to an end. It almost killed her when your father died. She went crazy. I tried to stop her from taking you away and joining one of them strange religions up in some rainforest in New South Wales or Queensland or somewhere."

"We went to Mullum," said Kelly. "I didn't mind that. It was okay there. But we were always moving on."

"Well, you're welcome to stay here," sad Gramma. "No need for you to keep moving on now."

"But I have to find her."

"You could stay for at least a few days."

"I want to go to Hobart. I think she's there."

"You'll have to stay at least for tomorrow," insisted

104

Gramma. "The families come on Sunday. You ought to meet your uncles and their families."

That night Kelly slept in the same room she had slept in when she was a little girl. When she emptied out her pack, Gramma said, "That lot wants washing!"

"I did wash some of my clothes out," said Kelly. "But I left them on a clothesline at a caravan park."

"Haven't you got any pyjamas?" Gramma was searching through Kelly's few belongings.

"No. I didn't bring any."

"You must have left in a hurry," said Gramma as she bundled up Kelly's few pieces of clothing. "I'll put this lot in the laundry basket. It's lucky for you there's plenty of stuff here. The kids always leave things. They usually come here on holidays." She opened the cupboard. "Here! Katrina's things should fit you. She's grown out of these." Gramma pulled jeans and other things out of the cupboard. "Don't suppose you remember Katrina. You used to play together. She's about your age, but bigger than you now." She put a pair of clean, neatly folded pyjamas on the bed. "You can put these on. But get a shower first."

"I had a shower today," said Kelly. But it seemed such a long time ago.

"You don't look as if you had," said Gramma. "You look real scruffy to me."

Freshly showered and dressed in clean pyjamas, Kelly snuggled down in her old, soft bed, and slept soundly all night. And the old dog slept at the foot of the bed.

14

The peace rally was over. It had not been a great success. About two hundred people had turned out, almost half of them children. The only television camera there had *not* been from the ABC.

"Of course the churches are having special services of their own tomorrow," said Allie.

"To keep the faithful from being contaminated by us lot, I suppose," said Katie.

The two women were walking home together. Katie's feet were sore, her voice was hoarse, and the baby was whining in the back pack. Allie had a headache and a feeling of being fed-up with everything. To get rid of Mick and Mandy she had given them money to go to the pictures. She was wondering why life was always such a struggle. Why wasn't there someone to look after her, to take care of her?

"It looks as if your friend Peg has fallen on her feet, anyway," Katie said.

"Yeh." Allie grunted. "And then going on at me as if it was my fault Kelly has gone off."

"I liked that big fellow, Con Carmondy," said Katie. "I wouldn't mind finding somebody like that."

"Yeh," Allie grunted again.

"I could be a traitor to feminism right this minute," said Katie, "if I could find some big, soft bloke like that to look after me."

Of course it was Fred Towns who had arranged for the Carmondy Country Folk to be at the rally. Trust Fred to do none of the hard work and then make the big gesture, Allie thought. Fred had asked the Carmondys months ago, before their success began the meteoric rise claimed for the group by the pop publicity of the local press. Their popularity, which had been rising steadily but unspectacularly for months, had taken an upsurge recently with the addition of the new singer, Peg Ryan. Remembered, said the publicity, as one of the popular duo of the late sixties and early seventies, Peepee Ryan, Peg brought a feminine (some said feline) quality to the previously male trio. Backed by the plaintive music of guitar and violin, the voices of Peg Ryan and Con Carmondy, responding, blending, and overflowing with such intensity of feeling and sincerity, found an eager, even ecstatic response from every audience.

"How did Fred Towns get to know Con Carmondy, anyway?" Katie asked, enviously.

Allie shrugged. "Doesn't everybody in Tassie know somebody who knows somebody who eventually knows everybody? But Con Carmondy had something to do with Theatre in Education once, and Fred was a teacher."

"I've never seen him at a rally before."

"He's been to quite a few, but not up here."

"You usually see the same faces at all of them," grumbled Katie. "The peace, the environment, the anti-nuke lot. Nobody else cares. They'd rather be fried than make fools of themselves."

They had turned the corner, and Allie was glad to see

107

her own gate across the road, hanging on its broken hinges. "It's a pity, " she said, "that we didn't get some pre-publicity about the Carmondys coming."

"It'll be on telly tonight."

"But we needed it beforehand. That's what I told Fred, and she said she didn't think they'd come. Although she asked Con ages ago, and he agreed then, she hadn't heard from him lately. And she wasn't able to get in touch with him. The group's been pretty busy just lately. Fred says she was as surprised as anyone when they actually turned up."

"And what did you think about finding that Kelly's mum was their lead singer?" asked Katie.

"Cats always fall on their feet," said Allie.

Con Carmondy always said that he kept his promises. His way of life, personal and professional, was based on a simple, practical sincerity. To Peg, whose life had been one long search for an illusion to disguise the truth about herself, Con had seemed unbelievable. At their first meeting she thought his unaffected sincerity must make him painfully vulnerable in the sort of world he inhabited, but she soon saw how well protected he was by his own sound, discriminating judgment. Con Carmondy was no fool. He overwhelmed Peg as she had once overwhelmed the young Patrick Ryan with her weird obsessions about a mystical, musical way of life. But Con's influence over her was different, not based on some mad dream, but on his artistic understanding of her small but eloquent talent, and her desperate need for some certainties in her casual, heedless, increasingly hopeless life.

So Peg had joined the Carmondy Country Folk, and within a week was the piquant ingredient in the Carmondy's new sound. And she loved Con Carmondy. She believed that everybody who met him must love this huge, gentle man. She wished she could be as open and frank with him as he was with her. She wanted to tell him the truth. *He wouldn't care,* she told herself. *It wouldn't matter to him.* But it mattered to Peg. She had left the truth about herself a long way behind. She had run away from it. She had become someone else, not just an invention of her own imagination but a different person, constructing her own life by her own standards. She had not always done this successfully, she admitted to herself, but she had done it independently, especially since Paddy Ryan's death. Con knew about Paddy, of course, and had admired him in his day. He knew, too, that Peg had a daughter. She had told him Kelly was staying with a friend. She had said they would probably meet Kelly and the friend at the peace rally. She had planned to surprise Kelly, and perhaps take her away with her again. It would be nice to have her daughter with her, she thought, now that she had something to offer her. It had come as a shock to her to learn that Kelly had left Allie's house and gone to a stranger, an old woman, who had had some sort of accident and allowed her to *disappear.*

"What about her grandfather?" she had asked Allie.

"What the hell do I know about her grandfather?" Allie had replied.

Fred Towns was bubbling over with news, and at the same time vexed with disappointment. She had scored a marvellous coup in getting the Carmondy Country Folk to the peace rally, but had missed out on pre-rally publicity. She hadn't told anyone she had invited the Carmondys for fear of being humiliated if they didn't turn up. But they *had* turned up, and Con Carmondy, that big, handsome bear of a man, had embraced her in public as though she was an old friend, and not just an acquaintance from years ago. The television cameras (unfortunately only the commercial station) had been *right there* to put it on film, too. It was bound to be on the evening news. Fred was *dying* to tell someone about it. Allie Jones had appeared completely unimpressed. Helen Hopper wasn't even there! And the Hoppers could not be expected to watch the *commercial* news. Maybe she should drop in on them on the way home, thought Fred, although the Hoppers, especially Lionel, always made it clear that they were not the sort of people one *dropped in* on. She could stop at the shop to see Timothy, of course, but Saturday afternoon was his busiest time. Maybe she should go the hospital and see Mrs Kneebone.

Did Mrs Kneebone know that Kelly had a mother, Fred wondered. Allie Jones had known. Well, of course, Peg Ryan had left Kelly at Allie's place. It was astonishing, thought Fred Towns, the way Allie seemed to accept as not worth mentioning the fact that Kelly had been *dumped* on her by a mother who, almost absent-mindedly it seemed, had moved on without her.

"I've got other things to worry about," Allie had said. "Like minding my own business. Anyway, things seemed to be working out all right between Kelly and Mrs Kneebone."

Well, thought Fred, at least Kelly had had the good sense to move out of Allie's house and in with Mrs Kneebone. But where had she gone now? Fred could hardly believe that Peg Ryan was really so upset when she found out that Kelly had disappeared. That was just pretence, surely. If she really cared so much about Kelly, why had she gone off and left her? And there was another thing! Peg had said she thought Kelly's *grandfather* would find her at Allie's place. And this so-called grandfather turned out to be Timothy's partner, old Mr Ryan! Well, what could you make of that? The old man had never mentioned a granddaughter, although Timothy had said he believed old Ryan thought he had a grandson somewhere. But, Fred decided she was not inclined to believe anything Peg Ryan said. She thought she was decidedly *shifty*. Look at the way she was hanging on to Con. She really had her claws firmly anchored there. And he'd had a big, protective arm around her, saying all the time. "It's all right, love. Don't worry, we'll find her."

The Carmondy Folk had left as soon as the rally was over. They had to get back to Hobart for an evening performance. Fred turned the car towards the antique shop. If Timothy was busy she could talk to old Ryan, she thought, and make discreet inquiries about his grandchild.

Ryan, however, was not at the shop. Timothy said he had gone to the hospital to see Mrs Kneebone. She tried to talk to Timothy but he had no time to listen.

"I'm terribly busy, love, tell me when I get home."

That meant that Helen Hopper was the only person left to talk to, but as Fred drove down Clare Street she saw the Hoppers had visitors. Big cars were parked in front of the house, blocking the street. In the end Fred went home and applied her energy to painting the old garden furniture she was restoring in the courtyard. She thought how she would have liked to arrange a luncheon or evening party for the Carmondy Folk. She would have invited Helen Hopper, even though the Hoppers never invited her to anything. She imagined herself saying to Helen Hopper, "I hope you'll come and meet the Carmondy Country Folk". Then she sat back on her heels and looked disapprovingly at the chair she was painting. Helen Hopper, she thought, would probably say, "Carmondy Country Folk? I don't think I know them." She was probably more into string quartets and Musica Viva.

At the hospital old Mr Ryan was sitting stiffly, uncomfortable in his best clothes, in a hard-backed chair.

"You didn't go to the peace rally?" said Mrs Kneebone.

"What peace rally?"

"It was on in the square today."

"Never heard about it."

"I thought Timothy Towns would have told you."

"He might have. I forget things."

Mrs Kneebone looked at the old man's thin, grey face. "How are you keeping these days?"

"No good complaining," he said. "But you're looking all right, better than I thought you would be."

"I'm feeling all right. I could be going home tomorrow or the next day."

"As soon as that? They kick you out pretty sharply these days, don't they?"

"Oh, I'm ready to go home." Mrs Kneebone was thinking that Mr Ryan hadn't worn too well, but then she didn't suppose she had worn any better. "It's been a long time," she said.

"It has," agreed old Ryan. "But after your Alec died there was the trouble with Dulcie. She was never the same after the boy left."

"I hear you've got a new business partner now."

"A new business! The old business was going downhill when Timothy Towns bought into it."

"Do you think he's honest?"

"Honest?" Old Ryan looked surprised. "Yes, I think so. Why do you ask?"

"He came to see me this morning with a policeman,

112

that nice new sergeant whatever-his-name-is, who said he was here *unofficially*. He showed me some things and asked me if I recognised any of them."

"Stuff from the shop?" asked Mr Ryan. "I know Timothy showed some stuff to the sergeant. *Did* you recognise it?"

"I said I didn't. I told the sergeant that I didn't."

"Yeh, but *did* you?"

"The sergeant wasn't suggesting that Timothy or anyone connected with the shop was engaged in dishonest dealings," said Mrs Kneebone, not answering the question. "I believe Timothy bought the stuff from Terry Jones, Allie's ex-husband."

"Before I bought any stuff from Terry Jones," said Mr Ryan, "I'd want to know where it came from. But young Towns doesn't know the people round here the way I do."

Mrs Kneebone was looking anxious. Of course she had worked out the connection between her stolen property and Terry Jones and the blow on her head, and even the possibility that young Mick might have helped his father in some way. But she was sure the little boy had nothing to do with the attack on her.

"I don't know Terry," she said, "but I know Allie and the children, and I wouldn't like to cause them any trouble." She would have a word with Mick privately, she decided.

"I reckon Terry's shot through by now," said Mr Ryan. "Timothy's been looking for him, but he hasn't been at the place where he lives, and there's some suggestion he's gone to the mainland."

Mrs Kneebone fumbled with the box of chocolates on her lap. Mr Ryan had brought them. It was a long time, thought Mr Ryan, since he had bought a box of chocolates and put on his best clothes for a lady. He had always liked Mrs Kneebone and was sorry when they dropped their friendship, but Dulcie had been very difficult at the end. Mrs Kneebone handed him the chocolates, and Mr Ryan selected a soft-centred one. Hard-centred ones pulled his dentures out.

"Kelly's coming back," said Mrs Kneebone.

"Good! She's a nice kid."

"I never knew," said Mrs Kneebone, "just how much you can miss not having children or grandchildren until Kelly came to stay with me."

"Having children of your own," said old Ryan, "is no great comfort to you sometimes."

"Oh, I know," agreed Mrs Kneebone. "Poor Mrs Swann. She's so upset about her grandson, Josh, running away."

"And don't forget that our boy left us," Ryan sighed heavily. "That was the end of Dulcie. She thought the sun shone out of him."

"He was a nice boy," remembered Mrs Kneebone. "In St Joseph's choir, wasn't he? Such a pleasant boy. Always singing, always happy."

"Dulcie spoiled him." Ryan grunted. "Our only child. One child, one chance. But I don't know if it makes any difference if you have six. You do what you think is best I suppose."

Mrs Kneebone thought about Ryan's son, Patrick. "Wasn't he a clever boy?"

"Oh, yes! Went to the university, studied sociology. That's when the trouble started. He began talking about things like 'changing awareness' and joined anti-war and anti-everything protests. *Dropped out*. Then there was Vietnam. He was a pacifist. He had this pop group. Very good, so everyone said. I don't know about these things. Then there was this girl. Her name was Peggy, and he started calling himself Paddy. They joined up together, called themselves *Peepee* Ryan. For Peggy and Paddy, you see? They weren't married, not at first. Maybe not ever. I don't know. She had a good voice, but she was a strange girl. We didn't really know her. She wore bangles and beads and bells and things. Talked about 'flower-power' and 'love-ins'. They had this new idea about 'soul' music. Popular, but *weird*. They burned incense at their performances and had these lights they called *psychedelic* or something. It was all very strange."

Ryan and his wife, Dulcie, had been completely confused by these changes in their son. They didn't know what to do. They felt helpless.

"When Patrick went up to the mainland with that girl, Dulcie was distraught," the old man went on. "She worried herself sick. Literally. Then the boy wrote to tell us he was in Sydney, in a place he called an 'urban commune'. It seemed to be a sort of boarding-house where young people, mostly what you'd call intellectual upper-class, lived together in what he termed 'sexual freedom'. That was just too much for Dulcie. She wrote back telling him she never wanted to see him again."

"And she never saw him again?"

"Never!"

"How sad!"

"But we had news of him, of course, and sometimes we heard him. We heard his songs, we heard him singing on the radio. Dulcie always cried."

Patrick — or Paddy — married Peggy, old Ryan told her, in some kind of ceremony up near the Queensland border under a Moreton Bay fig-tree. It was in the papers. Dulcie tore up the pictures. "Call that a marriage!" she'd wailed. But old Ryan had kept some of the pictures.

"At the end of the sixties," he said, "do you remember there was a musical called *Hair* on in Sydney? At Kings

Cross. Well, it would be at Kings Cross, wouldn't it? The performance ended with the cast coming naked onto the stage, dancing and inviting the audience to join them. The police arrested people."

There were headlines in the papers, he told Mrs Kneebone. Pictures. Things were printed about a 'tribal love-rock' and its message of *freedom*. One of the papers published a picture of Ryan's son. *Naked. It was there in the papers*.

"I thought Dulcie would go clean out of her mind," he said. "It was terrible! After that she wouldn't even *speak* of Patrick. She never saw him again."

Dulcie Ryan had died without ever seeing her son again. She had refused to allow anyone to let him know she was dying. Yet Ryan had made some attempt to let the boy know. "But I had no address to write to," he said. In the end he sent a letter to an old address, but had received no reply, not until after Dulcie was dead.

When the letter did come it was not from their son but from his wife, Peggy. By that time Paddy Ryan was dead too, killed in a car accident. There was no address on the letter. It was brief and bitter. It said the Ryans had rejected her and Paddy, and that they need not worry about her now. She said she and her child had plenty of friends to help them.

"I didn't know until then there was a child," Ryan said.

"Have you never seen the child?" Mrs Kneebone asked gently.

"No."

"Nor Peggy?"

The old man frowned. "I don't know. A couple of weeks ago I thought I saw her in the shop. I'm not sure. It's hard to remember what she looked like, and she'd have changed anyway."

"Didn't you speak to her?"

"She ran away. She just took one look at me and ran away. There was a child with her."

"Your grandchild, maybe."

"Maybe. But I think it was a girl, not a boy. It's hard to tell the difference, the way they dress these days."

"Is your grandchild a boy?"

"I've always thought of him as a boy," said old Ryan. "Someone like Patrick. But I don't know. I really don't know." He seemed to draw away into himself. He sat on the hard hospital chair and fell silent with his thoughts, upright and distant.

Mrs Kneebone leaned back against the pillows and closed her eyes. Her mind turned to Kelly. A moment later her eyes flew open. "Of course!" she cried. What an old fool she was, she thought. Why did it take her so long to think of things? "Peggy!" she cried. "Peggy Ryan!"

"What?" The old man jerked foward. "What's that?"

"That's her name!" Mrs Kneebone was clutching old Ryan by the hand.

"I know it is."

"But it's Kelly's mother!"

"What?"

Mrs Kneebone could remember clearly Mick standing beside her bed, saying, "*Peg . . . she's mad*!" "Don't you see?" She was shaking Mr Ryan's hand. "Peg Ryan — she's Kelly's mother!"

117

15

Kelly awoke on Sunday morning in the bright, sunny bedroom at Gramma's place. She thought, "Well, now I know a lot more about myself."

Was she happy with what she knew? She was not sure yet. She dressed and went out into a morning of rosy sunshine. The garden was dry. Even the raspberry canes were wilting. The breeze rustled through the leaves; grey ribbons of bark were hanging from the big gum-trees. Before breakfast Kelly walked down to the creek, passing currant bushes, and wild geraniums growing between rocks. On the bank the ground crumbled like stale biscuits. When she came back Gramma was waiting to have breakfast with her. Afterwards they went down to the vegetable garden to pick tomatoes and strawberries for lunch. Wherever Kelly went the dog, Jason, went with her.

Gramma's sons, Kelly's uncles Gary and Doug, came for lunch with their families. Gary's wife was Patty, and they had two children, Shane and Nancy. Doug's wife was called Sue, and their children were Greg and Jan. These two boys and two girls were younger than Kelly, but Shane at least was taller. They looked at her in her clean jeans, shirt and sweater.

"Hey! They're Katrina's clothes."

"Katrina's grown out of them," said Gramma. "They're Kelly's now."

"Well," said her Uncle Gary, walking round her and inspecting her with twinkling eyes, "so you're Peg's kid, are you? You don't look much like her."

"You must take after your dad," said Patty.

"Yes," said Sue, "your dad was small."

"Do you remember us?" Doug wanted to know.

Kelly shook her head. No, she couldn't remember any of them. Only Gramma.

"She remembered me," said Gramma. "Knew me as soon as she saw me. Didn't you, love?"

"Yes, I did."

And that was strange, thought Kelly.

"Gramma must have been pleased when you walked in," said Gary.

"Oh, yes! I was!" declared Gramma. She put her arm round Kelly. And now everyone was eager to touch her. They patted her shoulders, took her hands, kissed her. Kelly felt herself enfolded in the warmth of a family; *her family*.

Shane told her they had all been mutton-birding. "Have you ever been birding?" he asked.

"No, I haven't."

"*Never*?" The children were disappointed for her. "You could come with us sometime."

"Do you like mutton-birds?" asked Sue.

Kelly said she didn't know; she didn't think she had ever had a mutton-bird.

"You'll have some today," promised Gramma.

They had brought her some birds from their trip to the island. She pulled them out of the bag, admiring them, saying she had never seen better, not even last year's birds were better. She showed them to Kelly. Kelly didn't like the smell. When one was put on her plate for lunch she prodded it doubtfully with her fork.

Greg, the youngest of the children, was sitting opposite Kelly, across the big kitchen table. "We have a beaut time mutton-birding," he told her. "You should come sometime." He watched Kelly prodding at the bird. She saw him watching her. His eyes glinted, his mouth was greasy. His glance was scornful. "I betcha know nothin' about mutton-birding."

Kelly admitted that this was true.

"I know all about it," boasted Greg. "I've been heaps o' times." He began to tell her all about mutton-birding; how the birds were taken from the rookeries, killed, and carried spitted on long sticks. "Then you've gotta get the oil out o' them. You hold them like this." He demonstrated, holding up his bird. "The oil is squeezed out through the beaks."

Kelly dropped her fork. Gramma glanced at her face. "Stop that, Greg!"

"I was just showin' her!"

Greg finished his bird and asked for a second one. He watched Kelly still toying with her first. "If you come mutton-birding with us," he told her, "you'll hafta help. You could pluck 'em and cut the legs off."

Kelly pushed her plate aside a little. Greg grinned. "There's a lot you could do. Clean 'em and brush the down off."

Kelly watched the movements of his greasy lips.

"When they've been put on racks and dried they have to be opened and salted. But you wouldn't get the birds out of the rookeries or kill 'em. Girls don't do that."

"Women used to," said Gramma.

Kelly closed her eyes. When she opened them again, Uncle Gary was grinning at her. "Peg wouldn't go mutton-birding either."

"Wouldn't she?" Greg was surprised. "Didn't she like mutton-birds?"

"Why didn't she?" asked Jan, as if this was something beyond belief. She saw the bird still on Kelly's plate. "Don't you like 'em either?"

Kelly shook her head. She tried to explain without offending them: "You see, we're sort of vegetarians."

Uncle Doug snorted: "I'll bet that was one of Peg's damn-fool ideas!"

His wife, Sue, looked kindly at Kelly and tried to be reasonable. "Not everybody's the same."

"It would be a dull world if we were," said Patty.

But Greg stuck to the point: "Why are you a vegetarian?"

Kelly knew he wouldn't understand. "I guess we don't like eating animals that were living things, like us."

Greg dismissed that school of thought at once. "What about vegetables? They're growing and living, aren't they? It might hurt them when you pull them up, or cut them up and eat them."

"That's enough, Greg!" said Gramma. "You'll turn us all off our food!" She pushed cheese and salad vegetables towards Kelly. "You eat whatever you like, love."

After lunch the children went out to play. Kelly did not go with them because she didn't think she was a kid any more, but she watched them through the window. They had tied ropes in the big spreading branches of the two gum-trees, and were climbing up and sliding down. When they saw her watching they grinned at her, their eyes bright with mischief. They beckoned her out. At last she went to join them.

"You wanna climb up?"

She would like to try, Kelly said. The two girls showed her how easy it was, and it looked easy when they did it. But it was probably something they did every time they came to Gramma's, Kelly thought, watching how they used the trunks of the trees and the branches for footholds as they climbed. They slid down and landed at her feet. "You wanna try now?"

Kelly climbed up slowly, carefully, with the rope swaying out from the trunk of the tree and the ground getting farther and farther away beneath her. She had not realised the tree was so tall. She saw that Greg had started to climb the other tree. He made faces at her as he passed her, and reached the top of his tree while she was still only halfway. She was still on the way up when he screeched past her on the way down. Kelly was slow but stubborn. When she reached the top at last, she looked down and waved. The children below cheered. Then she saw that the worst part would be going down. She felt dizzy.

She began to slide on the rope from branch to branch, bracing herself against the tree-trunk. Suddenly, about halfway down, she felt the rope being pulled away from the main trunk. She began to spin, and felt her hands slipping and burning. She swung her legs wildly towards a large branch and managed to get a foothold. Gripping a higher branch in one hand and the rope in another, she looked down. She saw the three older children pulling the end of the rope away from Greg, and heard them shouting: "Don't! Stop it! You wanna make her fall?"

"You little shit!" she shouted down. "Wait till I get you!" She descended to the ground rapidly, without even thinking about it.

Greg ran away from her. He ran round and round the tree, shouting, "Ya! Ya! Ya!" and making faces at her as she chased him. He was fast.

"Just wait till I get you! I'll kill you!" she screamed.

Gramma stopped her. She caught her by the arm and grabbed Greg by the shoulder. "What's going on here?"

"He tried to kill me!"

"It looked to me," said Gramma, "as if you were hell-bent on killing him."

"No!" The other children all tried to explain at once. "It wasn't *her* fault, Gramma! Greg nearly made her fall!"

Gramma listened. She shook Greg by the shoulder. "Is that true?"

He admitted it was, and she cuffed him on the head. "You want to watch out!" she warned him. "Kelly's more than a match for you. Mind she doesn't do to you what she did to Aunt Fanny!"

Gramma went into the house again, warning them all to behave themselves, *just in case*.

Greg looked round-eyed at Kelly. "What d'you do to Aunt Fanny?"

Kelly said nothing.

"What did you do?" asked the other children.

"Nothing."

"Did you kill her or something?"

Kelly didn't answer. Greg began to dance around her. "You killed Aunt Fanny! Killed Aunt Fanny! Killed her! Killed her!"

"Shut up!" Kelly rushed at him, pushing him over backwards. Turning back to the house, she ran into Uncle Gary who was just coming out.

"What's the matter?" He caught her by the shoulders.

"Nothing."

"Are you all right?"

"I nearly fell out of the tree."

"Is that all? The kids are always falling out of the tree." Uncle Gary stepped past her. "Gramma says I should look at your bike. You want to come and show me what's wrong with it?"

"Okay." Kelly followed Uncle Gary to the shed.

"Did you come far on this?" he asked as he examined the bicycle.

123

"I've been on the road a couple of days. Since Thursday. I arrived yesterday. Gosh! Only four days since I left." It seemed like ages.

"You must have been riding pretty hard," said Uncle Gary. "Everything's a bit loose."

"I think I went in a big circle," said Kelly. She waited with Uncle Gary as he worked on the bike, handing him things from the tool-bag he had taken from his car.

"Try it now," he said when he had finished.

She rode the bicycle round the shed a few times. "It'll be fine now, thanks," she said.

But Uncle Gary was dubious. "Depends on how far you're going."

"I don't know. Peg could be in Hobart."

"In that case," advised Uncle Gary, "I'd ride in the other direction if I were you."

"I have to find her."

"Well, I suppose you know what you want to do. But Gramma would like you to stay here for a while."

"I could stay for another day."

"Is that all?"

"I want to find Peg. I ought to go tomorrow."

"Will you come back?"

"Yes! Of course I will!"

"Right. But don't forget to tell Gramma that," he said.

Patty waved from the verandah. "Afternoon tea's ready!" Uncle Gary waved back. "Coming!"

Kelly left the bicycle propped against the shed and went back to the house with him. The children ran in ahead of them, shouting. The table was set with cake and scones and biscuits, a big pot of tea and canned drinks.

"It looks like a party!" exclaimed Kelly.

"Maybe it is," said Uncle Gary. "For you."

When everyone had eaten as much as they could and more than they should, they all went and sat outside in the garden, in the shade, away from the sun.

"It's a late summer this year," said Gramma, fanning herself with the Sunday paper. The children clamoured for Uncle Gary to get his guitar and play some rock-and-roll for them. He said he was too full of tea to move, but eventually he gave in and went to get his guitar. Then he played and the children sang and danced and jumped around until Gramma said, "For heaven's sake stop it! It's too hot for all that!" Then the children flopped down and lay on the grass like rag dolls, and Uncle Gary strummed quietly on his guitar.

"Are you musical?" he asked Kelly. "Like Peg?"

"No," said Kelly, "not like Peg."

Uncle Gary sat quietly strumming away, but everybody else seemed to be falling asleep. "Kelly," he said after a while, "do you know this?" He played a few chords, then began to sing:

> *"I wandered through the mountains, and*
> *I wandered all alone,*
> *All through the valleys alone I did roam.*
> *I thought I saw the devil upon a mountain top,*
> *And I thought I saw God in a stream.*
> *The devil was a man with a gun in his hand,*
> *And the god in the stream was a dream.*
> *You say the man was reality, and the god but*
> *a dream,*
> *But I'll follow that vision down the mountain*
> *stream."*

At the end he turned to Kelly. "Do you know that one?"

Kelly shook her head.

"Your dad wrote that. A long time ago. Before he left Tassie for the mainland. Even before he met Peg."

"I've never heard it before."

"I always liked his early songs best," said Uncle Gary.

"Did you know my dad?" asked Kelly.

"Peg wouldn't let us get to know him." Garry began to strum on his guitar again. Everyone sat out in the garden until the sun went down and the night air began to turn chilly.

That evening, after everyone had gone home in Uncle Gary's truck, when Gramma and Kelly were sitting alone, Gramma said, "What do you think of your family?"

"I like them."

"But not mutton-birds?"

"No, not mutton-birds."

"You like the kids?"

"I don't know about Greg."

Gramma chuckled.

"But I like Uncle Gary," said Kelly.

"He's a nice man, Gary. He's like his dad," said Gramma. "Everybody liked his dad. He was drowned out fishing. A bad storm. People came from miles to say how sorry they were." She was silent for a while. At last she sighed. "It really upset Gary when Peg went off the way she did. He'd have done anything for his little sister. She hurt Gary more than any of us, I reckon. Like I said before, I always thought she was a silly girl and she'd grow up to be a silly woman. That's the way she was. I don't think you're gonna be like her."

Kelly didn't know what to say. Had she not run away, too, from Mrs Kneebone? Wasn't that a pretty silly thing to do?

16

By the time Mrs Kneebone left the hospital, she had made up her mind about a lot of things. In spite of her problems she felt brighter; even colours seemed brighter, and contrasts sharper. She seemed to experience everything more intensely. She thought it must have been the idea that she was going to die that had caused this change in her. For a while she had thought that life was slipping away from her. The strange thing was that this prospect of death made her think about life, and not without regret. She looked at the moon in the sky and the sunlight in the garden outside the ward window, and wept silently for her old bones in a lonely bed.

"But I haven't lived!" she cried to herself.

It was then that she resolved to make changes in her life. If she got out of hospital alive, she thought, she would *go on living*. Really living!

"You'd better take things easy at first," the doctor had warned her. But as soon as she arrived home she began to clear things out of the house. To give her more room, she said. She got rid of the big table and balloon-back chairs to make more room for the piano and the old armchairs, and for her friends to come and sit. The china

127

cabinet was full of bric-a-brac she didn't need, and there were ornaments everywhere that always needed dusting, and silver that needed polishing. Her head reeled when Timothy Towns had told her the sort of prices she could expect for some of these things. She had an interesting discussion with young Mr Towns. She had acknowledged that the things he had bought from Terry Jones had belonged to her, but said she didn't want to involve the police or make trouble for anyone.

"That wouldn't be nice, would it? Not for Allie, who has enough to cope with, nor for Mandy, or young Mick who is a nice boy when you get to know him, quite sensitive underneath."

Anyway, it seemed that Terry had suddenly disappeared. Gone to the mainland, they said.

"And good riddance too," said Mrs Kneebone. Any further association with his father would be a bad influence on young Mick, she thought.

Mrs Kneebone also decided to do something about Mrs Swann. The poor woman didn't look happy. She was upset about the disappearance of her grandson, Josh. What a lot of people seemed to be disappearing lately, thought Mrs Kneebone.

"I'm thinking of selling some things and seeing a bit of life," she told Mrs Swann.

"Oh, *I* couldn't do that!" said Mrs Swann. "I couldn't think of selling my things."

"Why not?"

"What would my daughter and son-in-law say?"

"Does it matter?"

"They prize those old family things."

"Then give them the first offer. Let them buy them if they want them."

How could Mrs Kneebone talk like that? Mrs Swann was appalled, but next day she began to think about it.

"We could have a nice time together," said Mrs Kneebone.

Mrs Swann couldn't remember when she had last had
a *nice time*.

Mrs Swann began to envy Mrs Kneebone. A few weeks
ago she had felt sorry for her, because she had been a
widow for so long and had no children or grandchildren
or any of the *advantages* that Mrs Swann had. She had
felt sorry and a little superior; she herself had received
so many blessings from God. Since Josh had left, however, she had begun to look more critically at her family.
What had they done for her? They had looked upon her
as a baby-sitter and someone keeping an inheritance in
safe keeping for them. And she wasn't sure that God
had been very active on her behalf, either. She missed
Josh. The boy had been her favourite.

"It's a dreadful worry," she admitted to Mrs Kneebone. "Even talking to the Reverend Harwood didn't
help."

"Children are the victims of the times," Mr Harwood
had told Mrs Swann. He painted a chilling picture of
what he called 'the youth rebellion'. Mrs Swann didn't
understand much of what he said, but she didn't like it.
Anyway, Josh wasn't like that. He never dressed in those
black and grey doomsday clothes. He wasn't like those
boys who shaved their hair at the sides and brushed it up
in stiff bristles on the top of their heads. She wondered
if they realised how frightening and yet how sad they
looked.

"Of course they know," said Mr Harwood. "They want
to frighten and worry us. They do it on purpose."

"Why?"

"Don't you think we frighten them? Look at the future
we've given them. The bomb. Power politics. Unem-

ployment. Of course, we've frightened them. And they see through our cruelty and greed."

Mrs Swann had wanted to protest. She had never been cruel or greedy in her life. But of course she wouldn't argue with Mr Harwood, and so he went on, explaining to her the sin of the world; the blackness which to young people was like a black hole in their universe, a vortex of nothingness. It sounded dreadful to Mrs Swann, and it would have sounded worse if she had had a clearer idea of what he was talking about. It seemed to her like a new slant on the old doom and damnation theories. But Mr Harwood was a good man, she was sure of that. He was lively and genial — in spite of what he actually said — and he got on well with young people, as if he understood their despair in his own jaunty, never-say-die way. If he thought Josh was like those other boys he spoke about, however, she was sure he was mistaken. Josh wasn't like that. With his soft, floppy hair, dressed in collarless shirts and tight jeans, he always reminded her of Oliver Twist. He had never been a *clever* boy, but he had seemed happy. Her daughter and son-in-law had put too much pressure on him to do well, to be always an achiever at school and sport. Lately she had been sure he wasn't happy. He had grown secretive and withdrawn. She wished she had tried to talk to him.

Mrs Swann took Mrs Kneebone home from the hospital in her mini. When they turned into Clare Street they were surprised not to find Fred Towns watching for them. Mrs Hopper was there, however, polishing a new brass nameplate on her front gate. She waved. "Welcome home!" she called.

"She's very friendly," said Mrs Swan.

"Yes. She came to see me in hospital," said Mrs Kneebone.

"You must have had people in and out day and night," Mrs Swann observed, a trifle sharply.

Mrs Kneebone seemed to have a lot of friends lately, she thought as she made a pot of tea in the kitchen. "I don't suppose you really *needed* me to bring you home," she said.

"But I'm so glad you did!" said Mrs Kneebone. "We'll have time for a chat." She told Mrs Swann that she thought Helen Hopper was *fishing for business*. "Mr Hopper has bought that row of old terraced houses at the bottom of the street. They're very rundown and past renovating, he says. So, he's going to pull them down and put up some nice new townhouse units for the elderly. Something tasteful, he says, in keeping with the street. And practical and convenient so that they'll be practically no work to do, and no garden to worry about."

Mr Hopper had said that if Mrs Kneebone was interested he was willing to buy her old cottage at a 'good price' and let her have one of the new units at a 'very reasonable figure'.

"I'm not surprised Hopper's got his eye on this place," said Mrs Swann. "A good, sound little cottage, so near their own place. It would do up nicely."

"Anyway, I dismissed the whole idea of selling up and moving," said Mrs Kneebone. "I said units might be all right for *old* people, and I might think of it then. But I'm only in my sixties"

"*Only* in your sixties! What did he say to that?"

"He hasn't given up. He acknowledges that nobody in their sixties could be regarded as old these days, but he advises me to 'keep it in mind'.

As the two women sat and sipped their tea, Mrs Kneebone said, "I was feeling much older a few weeks ago. That knock on the head must have done me good. I feel

131

quite young now. I won't say *again*, because I don't think I ever felt young before. I never looked *forward* to things."

"What are you looking forward to now?"

"Doing more. Getting about a bit more. Travelling. Not overseas. Well, not at first. There's a lot of Tasmania I haven't seen yet."

Once again Mrs Swann felt a twinge of envy. "That'll be nice for you."

"Why don't you come with me?" Mrs Kneebone asked suddenly.

"Me?" Mrs Swann couldn't believe her ears. "Oh! you don't want me with you!"

"Why not? We're friends. We've known each other for a long time. I enjoy your company."

"Really?" Mrs Swann was flattered.

"Do you enjoy mine?"

"Yes," said Mrs Swann. "Of course I do."

Mrs Kneebone thought she sounded a little uncertain. "Well," she said. "I suppose you have to be careful when choosing a travelling companion."

"Yes," agreed Mrs Swann, thinking it over quickly. "You'd be travelling in Tasmania?"

"To start with," said Mrs Kneebone.

"Well!" Mrs Swann made up her mind suddenly, and before she could change it again, she said, "We could go in the mini."

"That's an idea!" Mrs Kneebone was pleased and surprised. "Of course I'd help pay the expenses."

Suddenly aware that she was throwing caution to the winds, Mrs Swann raised her cup of tea in a salute to her old friend. "Watch out, Tasmania! Here we come!"

Both women laughed, and reached out and touched the brims of their cups together.

"Here we come!" they repeated.

17

In the morning Uncle Gary came over to Gramma's house in his truck. "I'm taking you into Hobart," he told Kelly.

"No need for you to take me," she said. "I can ride the bike. It's good now. You've done a good job on it."

Without argument Gary picked up the bicycle and put it in the back of the truck. "Throw your stuff in the back as well," he said. "I'm going into Hobart anyway."

"I don't know why you want to leave so soon," Gramma grumbled to Kelly.

"I have to find Peg."

"Don't see why. She should be looking for you. But she's not, is she?" said Gary, taking Kelly's pack and throwing it into the back of the truck. He climbed into the front. "Come on."

"Wait a minute!" Gramma looked at Kelly and straightened her clothes, pulling down her T-shirt and pushing two five-dollar notes wrapped in a list of names and addresses into the back pocket of her jeans. "Now don't you go sleeping out any more."

"I won't, Gramma."

"Plenty of people you can call on who'll look after you."

"Thanks." Kelly pulled herself up into the truck beside her uncle.

"Keep in touch."

"I will!"

"Wonder what your mother'll say about you coming to see us," said Uncle Gary as he drove towards the city.

"I don't care what she says, I'm glad I did."

Gary laughed. "You sounded just like Peg when you said that. She used to say, 'I don't care what anyone thinks, I'll do what I want!' "

"I'm not like that, am I?"

"Aren't you?"

What was she like, Kelly wondered. She had never thought about it. She was not a child, not yet grown-up. If she wasn't like Peg, who was she like? She sighed loudly. She felt like nobody, nowhere. She felt like the only one of her species. "Maybe I'm unique," she said.

"Unique!" Uncle Gary laughed. "Nobody is."

"Everyone is," declared Kelly.

Before he left Kelly in the middle of the city, Uncle Gary said, "Looking at it from Peg's point of view, I can't see why she dumped *you*, although I can understand why she dumped *us*. Aunt Fanny was one big reason."

"Aunt Fanny! Why?"

"Peg never could stand Aunt Fanny. And Fanny used to say Peg had 'ideas'. Peg was pretty and had some talent. She was set to *go places*. She reckoned Aunt Fanny spoiled things for her. I suppose she reckoned we all spoiled things for her."

"How?"

"By insisting on being what we are. By insisting on our existence the way we do. It's funny, you know, now everybody's running around like headless chooks trying to prove they're *real* Tasmanians, going through ar-

134

chives to prove that they're fifth- or sixth-generation Tasmanians, descended from convicts or first settlers or whatever. And here we are, descended from convicts, first settlers, sealers and whatever, and *thousands of generations* Tasmanian, but they don't even want to know about us. They try to convince themselves we don't exist. So *we* have to prove we *do* exist, and keep on proving it every day. That used to make Aunt Fanny really mad. And it made her sad, too. She solved both problems by drinking."

"And Peg?"

"Peg had a different problem, an individual problem. How to be herself. It's not easy for anybody growing up in a society that picks you out as an Aborigine, then denies you the right to be an Aborigine, and says you're nothing, *nobody*. And Peg badly wanted to be *somebody*. I remember Aunt Fanny saying to her, 'You're one of our mob whether you like it or not,' and Peg answering back, 'I'm not one of *any* mob!' She went off by herself and got a job as a singer. She got in with some strange people, and nothing we said could make her come back. When she met Paddy Ryan and joined up with him and went up to the mainland we thought that was the last we'd see of her. Then one day she turned up with you, and asked Gramma to look after you."

"Why? If she didn't want to have anything to do with you, why did she leave me with Gramma."

"She knew how well Gramma'd look after you. And you were only a baby. She wanted you looked after properly, I guess. She was living a fast life then."

Kelly thought about the things Uncle Gary had said as she pushed her bicycle through the Mall, dodging the shoppers who were hurrying or sauntering in and out of arcades and department stores. Other people were sitting in the sun, waiting and watching, eating out of

135

paper bags, listening to transistor radios or the busker with the violin in a sort of subdued carnival atmosphere of petty commerce. In her pocket Kelly had the address given to her by Chris, the puppeteer.

When she arrived at the address she found an old, shabby house, double-storied and set back in a narrow garden. The door was opened by a very thin, middle-aged man with a thick mop of grey hair hanging over his forehead, partly concealing his eyes.

"Yeah?"

"Chris gave me your address."

"Chris?"

"The puppeteer."

"Oh, lord! *That* Chris!" With a gesture of exasperation the man moved as if to close the door.

"He said you might be able to help me," said Kelly, putting out a hand against the door.

"Sorry, kid! No room! If I've told Chris once I've told him a hundred — a *thousand* times — he can't keep on sending people here."

"I don't want to stay!" cried Kelly, desperately.

The man held the door ajar, opened it a little more. "If it's money, we're right out of that as well." He peered at her through his flopping hair like some kind of sheepdog. "We *can* give you a feed, though. Gina got a case of over-ripe tomatoes from someone and she's cooking up some kind of Italian miracle in the kitchen." He moved aside to let Kelly come in. "But when the word gets around," he said, "and the word will get around, God knows how many we'll have to dinner! Still, it's first in, first fed, so come on! But leave your bike out there."

Kelly followed the man, a loose-jointed scarecrow figure in baggy trousers and T-shirt, down the hall and through to the kitchen, where a woman of about the same age but more ample propertions was working among the rich aromas of onions and tomatoes.

"This is Gina," said the man, standing beside the woman. "And I'm Jon without the aitch. Who are you? Haven't seen you before, have we?"

"No. I'm Kelly."

"She's a friend of Chris," Jon told Gina.

Gina threw up her hands. "Everybody in Tassie must be a friend of Chris!"

"I'm not exactly a friend," said Kelly. "He gave me a lift and your address."

Gina shook her head. "That's our Chris!"

"I'm looking for somebody."

"Sure, sure, sooner or later you'll find everybody here."

"Well, I've got work to do," said the man. "I'll leave you with Gina." He went out through the back door.

"You can give me a hand, if you like," said Gina.

As she sliced tomatoes, Kelly explained, "I'm looking for someone Chris said you might know about, or know where I can find them."

"Who?"

"The Carmondy Country Folk, or Con Carmondy."

"You're looking for Con?"

"Actually I'm looking for Peg Ryan. I'm her daughter."

"You're Peg's kid? You don't look much like her."

"I suppose I look more like my father, Paddy Ryan."

"Paddy! Yes, I remember him." Gina studied Kelly for a moment. "Yeh, you're a bit like him. He was small. A nice guy. Con's a nice guy, don't you think?"

"I don't know Con."

"Don't you? Well. You're mother's stuck on him, you know. And I reckon he's got it bad as well. Yeh, they've got a big thing going there. All of a sudden. Love at first sight, the second time around, and all that. Know what I mean?"

Kelly didn't know what Gina meant, and she didn't know what to say. Gina tipped the sliced tomatoes into a big pot. "So, you've never met Con?"

"No."

"Well," said Gina decisively, "we'll have to do something about that. Tonight, after dinner."

While Gina prepared dinner, she talked about herself and Jon and their house. It was a large house. In its better days it must have been a 'grand' house, but now it was showing signs of age and neglect. Gina referred to it as 'the hostel', and said that students on grants and young people on the dole found it a cheap and convenient place to live, although it had no official connection with any college, university or welfare department. In fact it was frowned upon by all official institutions (and its neighbours) as a den of delinquency. This was not true, nor could anyone prove it to be true, although efforts had been made in that direction, So Gina and Jon carried on the business of running the 'hostel' and offering somewhat overcrowded accommodation to the young and the homeless in a free and caring if rather disreputable community.

"We manage to make a living out of it as well," said Gina. "If you could call what we do *living*."

The house had been in Jon's family for generations, Gina said, and added: "They used to be merchant princes of Hobart."

Kelly thought Jon looked like a prince in a way; at least when he was sitting down or standing still; he was more like a clown when he moved. Immobile, however, he had an almost regal air, tall and thin, with a smile that blossomed on his sombre face like a royal blessing.

Before dinner the crowd had begun to gather in the

138

house, running up and down stairs, in and out of rooms, congregating in the hall, drifting into the kitchen, talking, laughing, greeting one another. It was mostly made up of young men, with one or two young women in their late teens or early twenties. Kelly wondered how they would all fit into the kitchen where they were to have their meal. Those who could found places at the long table, and others perched on stools or stood at benches. Two or three sat on the floor, pressed against the wall. One of these was a boy who looked familiar to Kelly. His soft, pale hair fell across his forehead. He had a wide mouth and high cheekbones, and his grey eyes looked around shyly, hesitantly, as if uncertain of his right to be there. He wore a collarless shirt, narrow faded jeans and canvas shoes. When he smiled at her Kelly was sure she had seen him somewhere before, but couldn't remember where. She was helping Gina to serve the meal. When the boy had eaten all that was in his bowl he handed it back, like Oliver Twist, and asked for more.

"Do all these kids live here?" Kelly asked Gina.

"No, we can only take three to a room, but they bring friends. And if somebody turns up with a sleeping-bag or blanket, how can you turn them away? Where can they go?"

When they were stacking up the dishes, Gina told Kelly they were going off to see the Carmondy Folk. "Leave the washing up. Let the others do that, we got the dinner ready."

Jon did not go with them. "I've too much to do," he said. He brought the old bomb of a van round from the back of the house for them and waved them off. Looking back at him standing on the pavement, paper-thin, almost fluttering in the breeze, Gina said affectionately,

"Bless the silly old pet! Works twenty-six hours a day and gets nothing done."

Kelly was still wondering where she had seen the *Oliver Twist* boy before, but when she asked Gina about him, she didn't seem to know who he was.

Then Kelly began wondering about Peg and what she would say to her when she saw her. She already knew the answers to a lot of the questions she had wanted to ask her mother. She knew some of the reasons why they had gone away, although she couldn't understand them properly. And, why had Peg gone and left her with Allie? And what had happened to Aunt Fanny?

Gina took Kelly to a crowded, noisy pub.

"I think I'm under age," said Kelly.

"It's at the family bar," said Gina. As they searched for a place to sit, she said, "Not a bad crowd for a Tuesday. But of course, this is the group's last week here."

"Last week? Where are they going?"

"Melbourne?"

"For good?"

"It'll be good for them, I reckon. Con says they want to spend the winter on the mainland."

So, thought Kelly, Peg had planned to go away without even telling her.

"I don't think I want to stay," she said.

"Course you do! Wait till you hear the music!"

Gina had bought a lemon squash for Kelly and a beer for herself. She had found a table and a couple of seats near the wall. "You know, your mum's lucky," she said, settling down. "You needn't worry about her."

"I'm not. And she's not worrying about me."

Gina, it seemed, did not hear her. "Yeh," she said, "Con's a real nice guy. Wonderful guy. The way he helps the kids that come to us. Generous — you wouldn't believe it!"

Kelly swizzled the straw in her glass. "How is he going to help them on the mainland?"

"Oh, he will! He says he won't forget us on the mainland. And he'll be back. Peg's got herself a real nice guy there."

Kelly scarcely recognised Peg when she saw her. Her mother had changed. She came out smiling, with shining hair and eyes, dressed very simply, without ornament. Her performance, too, was different, polished and graceful. Kelly thought this couldn't be the same Peg whose untidy, other-worldly incompetence had dragged them through odd places and religions, along free-floating hippie trails to folk festivals, alternative communities, and through all the muddles and hang-ups accumulated on the way.

"Con's made a big change in her," said Gina.

Peg looked very tiny beside the big man, beside the three big men of the group. As they sang together her clear, sweet voice soared above and blended with Con's softer, deeper tones. Before that first bracket of songs had ended, Kelly could see that more than Peg's appearance had changed. Her slight, graceful talent was so cleverly augmented by the Carmondy group that she seemed dazzling.

"She's good," she admitted, and joined in the clapping as loudly as anyone. It was then that Peg saw her daughter there. She stared in amazement until Con took her by the arm and led her off.

"Of course I wasn't going to leave you behind!" Peg declared later, in the little room she was using as a dressing-room. "I've been trying to find you. I said I wasn't going until I found you."

When Kelly had first walked into the room, Peg had

flung her arms around her and hugged her. "Gee! I'm glad to see you, love! I've been so worried about you!"

Kelly had drawn back. "Why did you leave me with Allie?"

"Because of your grandfather."

"*Who*?"

"He came running after us at that shop, remember?"

"My *grandfather*?"

"He followed us! I'm sure he did! I thought he'd come and find us. I didn't want to see him again. But I thought, if he finds you . . . well, I thought it might be a good thing. After all, *I* wasn't a very good thing, was I? Of course, I couldn't see the way things were going to suddenly change the way they have."

"When they did change, why didn't you tell me?"

"I tried to. I was going to surprise you. We went up to the peace rally. But you weren't there. Allie said you'd gone. She told me some old woman had been mugged, and you'd gone. Kelly! What happened?"

Kelly didn't know where to begin. "Where did you look for me?" she asked. "Did you go to the police?"

"Yes, we went to the police yesterday."

"Why didn't you go before that?"

"Kelly, the rally was on Saturday! Yesterday was *Monday*. We spent all day Sunday trying to trace you, phoning everyone we could get in touch with who'd been to the folk festival or anywhere you'd been lately."

"You didn't think of Gramma?"

"Gramma! Why would I think of Gramma? You haven't seen . . . I mean, not for years . . . *Have you*?"

"I was there, at Gramma's, yesterday."

"I never thought!" Peg looked at her daughter. "Hey! We've got a lot to explain to one another."

At the end of the evening's performances, Peg and Con went back with Kelly to Gina's house. They talked into the early hours of the morning.

"Why did we run away from Gramma's?" asked Kelly.

"Didn't *they* tell you?"

"Gramma said you were ashamed of them."

"Not of *them*, of *myself*. I thought I'd never be anything but what I was if I didn't get away from there."

"Was that so bad?"

"It wasn't what I wanted to be."

"That's what Uncle Gary said."

"Gary? He said that?"

"Yes. And he said it wasn't easy to have to prove you exist, and to go on proving it every day."

"Old Gary." Peg smiled softly. "He was always the wise one I'd like to see him again."

"Why don't you?"

"Yes, maybe. Why not?"

Gina had left them in the kitchen, saying, "Help yourselves to anything."

Con made coffee and sandwiches while Peg and Kelly talked. He was a big, gentle, bearded man, and he said very little, but sat and moved at ease, exuding warmth and patience.

"What about Aunt Fanny?" asked Kelly.

"Aunt Fanny!" Peg laughed, and then sang in a music-hall voice: "*Oh, my Aunt Fanny*."

"What happened?" said Kelly. She looked away, with the dread of some dreadful thing that had happened creeping like an itch under her skin.

Peg remembered, and laughed again. "You clobbered the old bitch with a garden spade!"

After a moment had passed, Kelly asked in a whisper, "Did I kill her?"

"Kill her? You were just four years old. You could

143

hardly lift the spade. I reckon you got her behind the knees."

"She fell!"

"Drunk!"

"Why did we run away?"

"I reckoned I'd had enough of Aunt Fanny, and so had you," said Peg. "Just about that time I'd had enough of everything, and I hadn't got over Paddy's death. I felt a strong need for the contemplative life, close to nature."

"At Mullum?"

"With the Buddhists," said Peg. "But that didn't work out either, did it?" She looked distracted and raked her fingers through her hair. She looked at Con. "I should warn you, sweetheart, things have a habit of not working out with me."

Con smiled, but said nothing. He set coffee and sandwiches on the table.

"You never talked about Aunt Fanny," said Kelly.

"Who the hell would want to talk about Aunt Fanny?" demanded Peg.

"I would."

"All right, go ahead."

"Who killed her?"

"I don't know." Peg looked puzzled. "But I can think of plenty of people who wanted to. When did you hear she'd been killed?"

"I thought . . . " Kelly hesitated. She shook her head. "I thought if it wasn't me it must have been you."

"*What*!"

"The arguments," said Kelly, "the screaming, the swearing at one another."

"She used to drive me mad. She'd drive anybody mad."

"You were fighting when I picked up the spade."

144

"I never thought you'd remember that."

"You said you wished she'd drop dead."

"Did I? I probably meant it."

"And she did!"

"What? Dropped dead?"

"She did, didn't she?"

Peg sat back and stared at her daughter. "I don't know what you're talking about."

For a moment Kelly had nothing more to say. She was distressed. She shuddered. Con was quick to enter the silence with the suggestion that any memory of what had happened when you were only four years old was likely to become confused in time.

"Then why did we run away?" Kelly asked Peg again.

"We left."

"You picked me up and ran away. You were crying. You were packing up and crying. You wouldn't talk, not to Gramma or anyone. We *did* run away," Kelly insisted.

Peg looked at her sadly. A gulf of misunderstanding widened between them. "I just *had* to get away. It was a bad time for me just then. I had to move on. Always moving on. But *you* never told me what you were thinking."

"*You* never wanted to talk about it — *ever*. You always said: '*forget it*'!"

"And so you thought we'd done in Aunt Fanny?" Peg shook her head unbelievingly.

"Something terrible happened," said Kelly.

"But not to Aunt Fanny. Not then, anyway."

"Then why did you never talk about it? You never said anything!"

"What was there to say? It was something we left behind us."

"Why did we never go back?"

145

"There was nothing to go back for. I didn't belong. I never belonged there."

"But I do!" cried Kelly.

Silence.

At last Con said, "Don't let the coffee get cold." Even Con felt that he wasn't coping with this. You could tell. They drank in silence, and began nibbling at the sandwiches. Kelly thought about what she had just said about *belonging*, and about her need to be a part of some intimacy, some relationship that was her own; a family, or a place.

"How did you find your way to Gramma's?" Peg asked at last.

"I just arrived there. It was as if that was where I was going."

"Are you going back there?"

"Not yet."

Peg took Kelly's hand. "Come with us!"

Kelly shook her head.

"We'd like you to," said Con.

"Come on!" urged Peg.

"I can't."

"Why not?"

"I have to go back to Clare Street. I have to see Mrs Kneebone again. And tell Mr Ryan I'm his granddaughter. And I have to return a bike somewhere. There's a lot of things I have to do. I'm not just a kid now, you know."

Con smiled. "Sweet sixteen."

"Soon be seventeen," said Kelly.

Peg burst into tears, and Kelly couldn't see why. Con leaned over both of them, large and comforting. "Hey! Come on! Kelly's not a kid any more. And it's not as if we're going off forever to the mainland. We'll be back in a few weeks. Before that, if you want to."

"I've been an awful mother!" wailed Peg, gripping Kelly by the hand. "But you will come and stay with us when we come back, won't you, love?" she pleaded.

"Sure," agreed Kelly. "Of course I will." She was wondering: just what *was* she going to do? She was confused by possibilities, and thinking about what Uncle Gary had said of the need to prove your existence every day. For the first time Kelly was beginning to experience some idea of her own existence.

18

"I don't know what to do," Kelly said to Mrs Kneebone when she came back to Clare Street.

"You can stay here," said Mrs Kneebone, "for as long as you like. Or with your grandfather. Only Mr Ryan wouldn't know what to do with you. Sometimes I don't think he knows what to do with himself."

Kelly tried to think of old Mr Ryan as her grandfather. They hadn't had much to say to one another, but she supposed they would get used to each other in time. It might have been better if she had been a boy; her father's son instead of her mother's daughter. Or Gramma's granddaughter. As it was, she was just a short kid with a mixed-up parentage and no special talent for anything. But that wasn't right either. She wasn't a kid any longer; she would have to make her own decisions about herself. That thought made her feel irritable and confused. It was better when she was just drifting along through life with Peg. Then, uncertainties had seemed perfectly normal. No one had expected her to make decisions about anything. Living in that pot-luck, casual way she had never had to think about what she was going to do tomorrow. Now everybody was asking questions. What would she do? Where would she go? Would she go to Gramma? Or stay with Mrs Kneebone? Or Grandpa Ryan? Or anybody? It was much easier when she had nowhere to go.

"Won't you come with us?" Peg had said.

"You can come with us any time," Con had added.

Mrs Hopper inquired, "Are you going back to work for my friend at the coffee shop? She'd be glad to have you back."

Too many options. It was worse than not enough. Kelly just wished everyone would stop prodding her with questions and suggestions.

"You ought to work at the shop with Timothy," said Fred Towns. "Your grandfather would like that. He can't work there for ever. He's getting too old already, and what is his will be yours one day."

But Grandfather Ryan said he didn't think Timothy needed anyone else in the shop. "But I suppose if I wasn't there, he might need you," he said doubtfully.

"Are you going away?"

"Well, I might be."

Timothy Towns told Kelly, with a wink, that the only thing that was stopping old Ryan from getting off on a trip was the thought of what the neighbours might say. "Otherwise he'd be heading off into a disreputable old age with Mrs Kneebone and Mrs Swann in Mrs Swann's mini."

Kelly didn't know if Timothy was joking. She asked Mrs Kneebone about it.

"I think somebody might have to knock him on the head first," said Mrs Kneebone.

And Kelly didn't know if *she* was joking.

Everything was changing so quickly it made Kelly feel dizzy. Why couldn't things stay as they were for a while? When she arrived back in Clare Street she'd found that

149

Mrs Kneebone had sold her big dining-table and balloon-back chairs, and had bought a new dress. Getting rid of some furniture made more room in the house, she said, and the dress was for Fred Towns' party.

"Are you going to sell *everything*?" asked Kelly.

"Of course not," Mrs Kneebone answered. "Only the things I can't be bothered with, that are just cluttering up the place." She looked at Kelly's face. "But if there's anything you want," she said.

"No," said Kelly. "Thanks, but there's nothing."

"Nothing?" Mrs Kneebone seemed disappointed. "Nothing at all?"

Fred Towns' party was to be held in the courtyard on Saturday. All week Fred had been worrying about the weather changing.

"What if it rains?"

"I can put up a tarp," said Timothy.

"We couldn't have everybody under a dripping tarp!"

"We won't be able to get the lot into the house," said Timothy.

Fred had invited *everybody*; every member and potential member of the Clare Street Community Project and all their friends. And *everybody* had accepted the invitation.

"Are ya goin' to the party?" Mandy asked Kelly.

"We're not," said Mick. "It's not for kids."

"What are you going to do?" asked Kelly.

"Stayin' home," said Mandy. "Lookin' after Katie's baby, 'cause Katie's goin' with Mum."

Kelly turned to Allie. "You're not leaving the baby with *them*?"

"Why not? They're not *lethal*," said Allie. "Not quite. Nor is their father for that matter, though I've spread the word that the cops are looking for him, just in case he's thinking of coming back from the mainland."

"But the baby!"

"Don't worry. My sister'll be here."

"Are you goin' to the party?" Mandy asked again, looking at Kelly.

"I guess so."

"Why? Are you grown-up now?"

Kelly shrugged.

"Are your gonna get married?" asked Mandy.

"What?"

"I'm not!" declared Mandy. "I'm never gonna get married. Katie says it's a mug's game."

Mick followed Kelly a little way down the street. "Wotcha gonna do with that bike?"

"Take it back, I suppose."

"Where?"

"Somewhere," said Kelly vaguely, "up the coast."

"Why don't ya give to me?"

"You?"

"Well, ya can't remember where ya pinched it, can ya? But if ya gave it to me, I could say honestly I didn't pinch it."

"You want to be careful," Kelly warned him, "or you'll turn out like your dad."

Mick stopped. He watched her walk on along the street. When she had gone a little way ahead, he called after her: "I never pinched nothin'!"

Kelly did not look back.

When Kelly had tried to explain to Mrs Kneebone about why she had run away, all her explanations sounded silly, even to herself. It was hard to recall the fear that had driven her away from Mrs Kneebone's house. Everything seemed to have been lost in her new insights and relationships. It was as if a new world had

151

opened up and swallowed her. Once there had been two drifters, she thought, Peg and Kelly, who looked after each other in a sort of a way, and didn't belong anywhere. Now it seemed that each of them belonged somewhere else, and Kelly didn't know where. It was as if she didn't know herself any more. She didn't know which decisions she ought to make about herself.

"But life is so exciting!" said Mrs Kneebone.

And *confusing*, thought Kelly.

"I have so many plans for the future!" said Mrs Kneebone.

Kelly couldn't believe it. She didn't know that anyone over sixty ever *thought* about the future. Kelly herself didn't want to think about it. She felt unsettled and confused, and it was the wrong time of the month for her. She was *cursed* in more ways than one, she thought.

The really strange thing was that Mrs Swann seemed the only one who really understood how Kelly was feeling. Mrs Swann had been thinking a lot about Josh lately, and the pressures young people were under these days. She had decided she was going to have a *straight* talk with her daughter and son-in-law about Josh. And about some other things. Of course, they wouldn't listen to her. Everyone had to learn for themselves, usually the hard way. She said to Kelly, "I don't suppose you saw Josh anywhere on your travels?"

"Josh?"

"My grandson. You saw him at the op-shop once, but you mightn't remember him. He's gone, you see. Run off."

Suddenly Kelly remembered. "Yes! Of course!" *That* was where she had seen him before — that *Oliver Twist* boy at Gina's and Jon's place.

"You did see him?" asked Mrs Swann.

"I reckon it was Josh."

"What was he doing?"

"Having his dinner."

"Dinner," said Mrs Swann. Well, it was a relief to know that he was eating. "What was he having?"

"Heaps of Gina's lasagna," said Kelly. "He had seconds." She laughed at the memory of the tall, shy boy, holding out his plate.

Mrs Swann breathed out a great release of anxiety. "Oh! I'm so glad. I must tell his parents."

But would his parents want to know? Of course they would! Although Mrs Swann thought they might not be as concerned as she was about what the boy was eating. They would certainly want to know about him and what he was doing. And whether he had given any thought to *them* and how *they* felt. Mrs Swann sighed when she thought of the life of complaint and irritation they led. There they were, middle-aged, in the middle of their petty lives, plagued by so many distractions they lost one experience in another. Just think of the pressure they had put on poor Josh! Once again she wished she had made an effort to talk to the boy. Probably he wouldn't have listened, but she should have tried. She was going to find him and talk to him as soon as possible.

"Listen," she said to Kelly. "Don't you rush into any decisions. Just take your time. You've got your whole life ahead of you."

"And don't you worry about Josh. He'll be all right," said Kelly, remembering suddenly, clearly, the awkward youth, all angles and bones and confusion, holding out a dish, begging for dinner, begging for friendship. "He's very nice," she said.

A beaming smile bloomed on Mrs Swann's round face. "Yes, he is! Such a nice boy!"

Peg telephoned from the Hobart Airport to say goodbye. "We'll only be away for a few weeks. Maybe a couple of months."

"See you when you get back."

"You'll come and stay with us?"

"Yeh," said Kelly. "Sure."

Peg hesitated at the other end of the line. "We've been to see Gramma."

"You and Con?"

"Yesterday."

"That's good."

"We told her we were getting married."

"You and Con?"

"Who else?"

Pause.

"Are you pleased?" asked Peg.

"Sure. I guess so."

Silence.

"Gramma sends her love. Says she hopes to see you soon."

"Sure," said Kelly. "Soon."

Then Peg talked to Mrs Kneebone for a moment. When she had hung up, Mrs Kneebone said, "Your mother sounds very nice, but a bit worried about you."

About time, thought Kelly. "She needn't worry," she said. "I'm all right."

"That's what I told her," said Mrs Kneebone. "Kelly's got her head screwed on the right way, I told her, she knows what she's doing."

What was she doing, wondered Kelly. She was going to the party at Towns' place. She was walking along the street with Mrs Kneebone. The last lingering summer sun was warm on her head and arms. All along Clare Street gardens blazed with colour and confusion and falling petals. But the season was turning, change was in the air. Kelly wondered where she would be next week, next month, next year. Not in Clare Street. She passed each house with a feeling of regret and expectancy. A couple of weeks ago she had felt abandoned, alone. She had found friends here in Clare Street, and then she had found a family. Now, she thought, she had to find herself. Who was Kelly Ryan? Where was she going?

Kelly was wearing the new dress Peg had bought for her when they spent a day together in Hobart, shopping. Fred Towns greeted her at the door of the courtyard with an exclamation of surprise.

"Kelly! What a lovely dress! It makes you look quite different!"

Kelly was not sure if that was a compliment, but she said *thanks* anyway.

"You look like a real young lady!" said Fred.

That was *not* a compliment, decided Kelly, and made no response.

Fred appealed to Mrs Kneebone, later, when the party was in full swing. "Don't you think Kelly looks like a real young lady?"

"She's grown up overnight," said Mrs Kneebone. She giggled because she was drinking a glass of champagne and the bubbles tickled her nose. Sometimes Mrs Kneebone thought that blow on the head had not only knocked her out, it had knocked her a bit silly. "Life is so exciting!" she said, gaily.

"I suppose you're excited too," Fred said to Kelly. "Finding you have a grandfather and grandmother and everything. And now your mother is getting married again. What are *you* going to do?"

"I don't know." Kelly shrugged. "I haven't made up my mind yet."

"I know just how you feel!" cried Mrs Kneebone. "It's so hard to make up your mind, isn't it? I simply don't know where I want to go, or what I want to do first."

Kelly was suddenly seized by a feeling of panic. She thought: *I hope I get it all together before I'm sixty!*

THE BRIGHT SPARKS FAN CLUB
WOULD YOU LIKE TO JOIN?

Would you like to receive a **FREE** bookmark and BRIGHT SPARKS friendship bracelet?

You are already halfway there. If you fill in the questionnaire on the reverse side of this page and one other questionnaire from any of the other BRIGHT SPARKS titles and return both questionnaires to Attic Press at the address below, you automatically become a member of the BRIGHT SPARKS FAN CLUB.

If you are, like many others, a lover of the BRIGHT SPARKS fiction series and become a member of the BRIGHT SPARKS FAN CLUB, you will receive special discount offers on all new BRIGHT SPARKS books, plus a BRIGHT SPARKS bookmark and a beautiful friendship bracelet made with the BRIGHT SPARKS colours. Traditionally friendship bracelets are worn by friends until they fall off! If your friends would like to join the club, tell them to buy the books and become a member of this book lovers' club.

Please keep on reading and spread the word about our wonderful books. We look forward to hearing from you soon.

Name _____

Address _____

_____

Age _____

You can order your books by post, fax and phone direct from:
Attic Press, 4 Upper Mount St, Dublin 2. Ireland.
Tel: (01) 6616 128 Fax: (01) 6616 176

Attic Press hopes you enjoyed **Mrs Kneebone and Me.** To help us improve the **Bright Sparks** series for you please answer the following questions.

1. Why did you decide to buy this book?
_____
_____
_____

2. Did you enjoy this book? Why?
_____
_____
_____

3. Where did you buy it?
_____
_____
_____

4. What do you think of the cover?
_____
_____
_____

4. Have you ever read any other books in the BRIGHT SPARKS series? Which one/s?
_____
_____
_____

If there is not enough space for your answers on this coupon please continue on a sheet of paper and attach it to the coupon.

Post this coupon to **Attic Press**, 4 Upper Mount Street, Dublin 2 and we'll send you a **BRIGHT SPARKS** bookmark.

Name _____
Address _____
_____

You can order your books by post, fax and phone direct from:
Attic Press, 4 Upper Mount St, Dublin 2. Ireland.
Tel: (01) 6616 128 Fax: (01) 6616 176